✳ The Designated Heir ✳

❋ Also by Maxine Kumin ❋

Poetry
HALFWAY
THE PRIVILEGE
THE NIGHTMARE FACTORY
UP COUNTRY: POEMS OF NEW ENGLAND

Fiction
THROUGH DOOMS OF LOVE
THE PASSIONS OF UXPORT
THE ABDUCTION

The Designated Heir

Maxine Kumin

The Viking Press * New York

908825

* For Janeo *

Part One

❋ 1 ❋

Buying the Child

"**Y**OU'RE HAVING a meat dream," he said.

They had just come from visiting the vealers. Every day they walked down Albert Muhner's barn floor and looked at each one of the little bull calves penned up at birth in wooden cages to fatten like Strasbourg geese. Usually they went in the late afternoon after knocking off work on the house they were building. The mortar grit would have caked on Robin's arms. Jeff would be stripped to the waist, his chest, floury with cement dust, striped now with drying sweat.

Today Muhner was late and the bawling had seemed demented. They never cried in unison, but at different pitches and in various phrases, so that you could pick out, for instance, the deeper sound of the little Jersey with the china-blue eyes and pink-mottled upper lip. A great rattle of crib slats and floorboards punctuated the lowing as the calves galloped in place in their pens.

"I can tell when you're having a meat dream," he said. That was how well he knew her, Jeffrey Rabinowitz, licensed architect, ex-Peace Corpsman, urban-housing dropout, her lover.

They were lying on their backs in the shallows, heads grating on the sand bar. Her small round body bobbed high in the water, Robin Parks of the Boston Parkses, hypocrite and glutton. His long pale frame rested on the bottom. Jeffrey Rabinowitz was a sinker.

Afternoons, as they watched, Muhner came in his high rubber boots and sloshed milk methodically from an open vat into the calves' nippled pails. One by one they fell to sucking the plastic teats, and their impatient feet that had never known the ground grew still. Then the barn was like a cathedral and the rhythm of nursing became a liturgy, and the manure that piled up like old yellow apples became an incense.

Afterward Robin always stood by the little Jersey and let him lap her fingers. His tongue was large and pale, a lolling sausage of sandpaper, and the sponge of his muzzle was warm and damp. Wherever she stroked him, his hide whorled in random patterns. The inner flap of his ears surprised her fingers.

On the way across the pasture down to the pond for their evening wash, she usually gagged. It was ridiculous because she was still a carnivore and Jeff, who kept his feelings to himself, was at least a vegetarian. Oh, she could go for a week on eggs and cheese and black bread and all the good bounty from the garden, but once the meat urge came on her, she could not keep her mouth dry. A hamburg, a steak, a slice of salami would rise up in her head like a painting and immediately she was awash with saliva.

So of course she had to swallow, but the taste—in today's fantasy it was roast leg of lamb sprigged with fresh mint from Sage's and served on her grandmother's silver platter—drenched her mouth again. The pink juice ran out under the carving knife and little beads of juice wetted the roast potatoes.

"It's so grotesque," she said. "I taste it and I smell it. I see me putting it in my mouth. I can feel my throat opening when I swallow. God! I just realized. I do everything but *chew.* "

She also picked her scabs and ate them. Probably he knew that, too.

"I wish you wouldn't feel so guilty about everything, Robinowitz," he said. She had never really had a nickname before, except with the family. They called her Binnie, which was predictable. But she was Jeff's Robinowitz. "I wish you couldn't feel so Christly guilty about a piece of meat. It's out of your control, after all."

She splashed a little for diversion. "You're such a thought monger. Living with you is like living with a psychoanalyst."

"You know what you do, don't you. You constantly pick up the most obvious thing and make some sort of miracle out of it."

"I don't know what you're talking about."

"Leg of lamb, for God's sake! You have an overdeveloped sense of wonder."

Had she said *lamb?* All her life she had silently reproached Gran and Tante—the grandmother and the great-aunt who had raised her—for a kind of obtuseness where her mind was concerned. Two previous lovers had not tampered with her private thoughts. And now she was reached into and explored daily and fistfuls of Robin unspoken came out into the light, all raw and wrong-way to.

"But with mint," she explained. "And potatoes."

"Cheer up," he said. "Aren't you happy?" And tenderly picked off a twig that had floated onto her stomach.

"The trouble with you is, you think it's your patriotic duty or something to be happy. So you never know if you are or not. That's your hangup, it's positively . . . Whitmanesque."

He laughed, drying his long, curly black hair. "But I *am*

happy. I'm happy with you." He scrubbed at his matching beard.

"Happiness is the absence of pain," she said.

What they did a lot of was argufy. All summer, rebuilding the stonework of an abandoned cellar hole into which the chimney had toppled, they squabbled in a comradely way. Was there a universal dormant consciousness? All summer, raising a new hearth from the heap of pre-Civil War bricks, squatting in the rubble, matching Jung and Norman O. Brown. She adored Erikson. He ridiculed Bettelheim.

The sills were beams from a barn that Muhner had torn down to make way for his new enterprise. The subflooring of remnants from the same barn was double-planked, and over it now they nailed roofing paper while they lived in the cave of the cellar. In isolation—satisfying or abrasive, and which was it at nightfall? Lumber for framing, men for raising were to come. It was to be a house of Jeff's own hands, a stubborn, old-fashioned house to go up where one had once stood in the Mink Hills of New Hampshire. The cleared land had reverted to scrub second-growth woods. On the five acres he owned, a good well had been left behind. When the settlers lit out for stone-free Ohio, they left also the apple tree and a tangle of lilacs as tough now as a thicket of gray birch.

Muhner was Swiss, a square man with ample biceps and clever hands. The day-old calves came, trucked in, packed nose to tail as neatly as kippers. Twelve weeks later they left in the slaughterer's van. A day of lime and disinfectant—Muhner ran a spotless operation—and another crop of newborns.

He had been in beef and capons and then sheep before the vealers. He was not unkind, nor was he a visionary; he fed and watered and mucked out as stolidly as if he were hoeing corn and when he spoke about himself it was of his youth in the canton of Valais. There at the local police station each Saturday the mushroom-hunters brought knapsacks of their foragings to be inspected and named, the steinpilz and chanterelles, and the great silky horse mushrooms that also abounded in his New World pasture. Whatever he thought of the young lovers he kept to himself. In the town they were called "those two hippies." Jeff heard it at the sawmill where he sometimes picked up a day's work loading lumber. It was also whispered at the grocery store. For this reason Robin seldom did the shopping. When she left Little Mink Hill in the Volkswagen bus she went in city clothes and with a city face clear to Boston to visit Tante and after Tante, Gran.

"Someday all these will be yours, Binnie," Tante said. They drank Dubonnet and gin, mixed half and half. Dust-free first editions of Edna St. Vincent Millay and Sara Teasdale and Edith Wharton were lined up over her head. The little apartment on Beacon Hill was stuffy, the Oriental rugs worn down to their essential warp and woof, and soot on all the window ledges. Tante's legs were so thin that the shins bowed outward a little above the stout, laced shoes. Robin could see her veins, a fretwork of purple, so trustingly pumping, sustaining. The Binnie that Tante knew was an English instructor vacationing in the country, visiting an old college chum, meanwhile preparing her syllabus from Chaucer to the Lake Poets for the fall semester.

"You have a fine mind, Binnie." Tante, who was fluent in four languages and despised Simone de Beauvoir. "A fine mind, you'll go far with it. When you get old you become keenly aware of your limitations."

When in fact Robin's mind was a stewpot. Yes, the mind of Robinowitz was a clutter of misconceptions and warring atti-

tudes. She had lived among the black flies with Jeffrey Rabinowitz for the entire month of June before she went to bed with
him. Others had preceded him. She was afraid that someone
would follow.

In the brownstone on Marlborough Street, dinner afterward
with Gran. From her she had inherited the family nose, which
sprang forth a little sharply from an undefined bridge. Thought
to be classical and in Binnie's case, small, in truth it was a
substantial nose. Gran, who favored long sleeves, favored also
a degree of décolletage and varied the chains that hung down
in the cleft so that she was constantly fishing something cold and
sharp out of its prison. Jade or gold or the cameo locket that had
been promised.

"My memories are portable, the best kind of baggage," she
said, applying the pincers to her lobster deftly so that the back
cracked clean across and her fork speared the tail meat whole.
Robin, less adroit, was guiltless. The fruits of the sea were part
of a natural rhythm; it was disposing of animal waste that
threatened the ecological balance. She sucked the thumb of a
lobster claw.

In the morning she could hear the calves bawling. She went
to the barn twice a day now. The little Jersey knew her. When
she rubbed his muzzle he rolled back his head in an appealing
way so that she could stroke the soft dewlaps that ran down to
his throat. He swayed with his eyes closed.

Muhner disapproved. "You oughta get a dog. A puppy,
now."

But she knew what she wanted.

Muhner took them on a chanterelle hunt. A mile downstream, wet to the knees with crossing and recrossing the same
quick brook, they found them, misshapen little yellow vases.

Cool and faintly waxy to the fingers with an irregular ruff of gills that ran down the stalk. Inside, they were chalk white. Muhner netted a dozen frogs and pithed them on the spot with the point of his knife. Something flickered across his face as he probed for the joint where thigh meets torso, then cut through and skinned the leg. He might have been rolling down a woman's stocking, the skin came away that simply. The remains he threw into the woods, frog faces on body skirts as limp as puppets. "Owls'll get 'em."

Later, Muhner's lantern bobbed along the path behind the barn. He had brought them six legs, all breaded and fried in butter laced with garlic. Robin thought she might eat one out of politeness. The meat was slippery and tender, moister than chicken. She gorged herself, finishing them all, then wiped the pan clean with a piece of bread.

Jeff watched.

"Thoreau ate meat," she told him. "He says somewhere he could have fried a rat or eaten raw woodchuck."

"He says a lot of things. 'I cannot fish without falling a little in self-respect,' remember that?"

"Frogs aren't fish."

"Frogs are worse. 'The gross feeder is a man in the larva state.' He says that, too."

She shuddered. She was reduced to a greedy child.

"And something about nations whose vast abdomens betray them."

She put her hands over her ears.

He relented. He patted her stomach. He liked it, little round belly full of frogmeat.

The chanterelles were delicious.

A work crew was required to raise the studding and tie in the ridgepole. Jeff had hired them from the sawmill. When they came, two redfaced men and an acne-scarred boy, she gathered up a load of wash and went into town in the bus. Either the men would bob their heads and call her Missus or they would not speak to her at all. She tried to think which was worse, the homage of a forelock tug, so to speak, or the ignominy of being put in Coventry. The nineteenth century was her field; she had been reading too much Hardy.

The Laundromat was housed in the old railroad depot. Hair piled up in a teacherly way, her long white neck exposed, she sat on a thickly varnished waiting-room bench and watched their clothes go around. It was not unpleasant, that steamy enclosed place of bleach and bluing.

People talked about them. She knew that, but tried not to listen.

"How do you know they're hippies?"

"Can't you tell? I know a hippie when I see one."

"I hear they're just living together in the woods up behind Muhner's place."

"Pretty soon they'll open up a commune. The whole town'll be full of them."

One by one she took the pins out of her hair and shook the bun free. She sat cloaked in straight black hair that fell to her waist. After a while the machine stopped spinning and the colors became once more the assorted towels, the faded jeans, the green, the blue, the two pale-tan turtlenecks of her experience.

The framing had gone up, as predicted, in a day. A week later the roof was on. She especially liked roofing nails with their flat wide heads, the seam of them making a line as tidy as thumbtacks on a bulletin board. There were to be four windows that opened and closed. Tomorrow they would buy a pump. There would be a sink next to the wood stove. She hammered left-handed, in a ragged rhythm.

"We could get married," Jeff said. "You could marry me, Robinowitz."

Closing in a house was a sacred act, she could understand that. To build was to dwell. But to put an imprimatur on all that traversing and measuring of space? She did not want the *Good Housekeeping* seal of approval. It would lead to central heating and carpets. It would lead to dusting and infidelity.

"The people who go to Laundromats don't have washing machines," Jeff said. "Don't you understand? They live in trailers with color TV sets. They have to have someone to feel holy about."

But that wasn't it.

"What *do* you want?" Jeff said.

What she wanted was beyond her saying. A light in the clearing, a sense of a plan. An immediate circle of beings to love and serve. She wanted to stay; she wanted also to leave him before the circle clicked shut like a combination lock. She wanted not to overhear the vealers' laments day after day. Whereas he had grown quite used to them. He did not hear the birds in the morning imitating distant and ineffectual machinery, and the calves' bawling in unison with the first light did not come to him like the cries of small damned children. Waking first, warming her cold nose in her palm, alone but grateful for his solid presence in the bed, she thought too much. Next week the calves would go to market. She had heard that they used to be stunned first with a sledgehammer blow between the ears. It was said to be humane. Nowadays they were electrocuted. Then their throats were cut and the blood collected in a trough.

It was a crop, like any other. She went off in the woods to gather mushrooms and took her find to Muhner in the barn.

"Puffballs," he told her. "Once in Switzerland I found one big as a man's head. You slice 'em like this and fry."

"How much will you get for the Jersey?"

"Depends. It goes by the pound."

"Fifty dollars?" The pump would cost eighty.

"Something like that. Forty, forty-two cents live weight. A Holstein'll go to two hundred pounds. But this little feller'll finish at one-fifty, maybe one-sixty."

She persisted. "Well, what is he worth today? Before he's finished? Fifty dollars?"

He knew what she was getting at. "You can't keep him long. Purty soon he'll be a bull and a bull is no pet. Ugly. He won't fetch you any price on the market once you put him to grass."

"I don't care what he'll fetch on the market."

Muhner shrugged. "Purty soon the grass stops growing, then you gotta feed him hay. Hay costs something, too."

But by autumn she'd have a steady income. An October paycheck. And Muhner would sell her the hay, she was sure.

"Look," she said. "If I give you fifty dollars tomorrow morning, will you let me take him away?"

Muhner's voice shot up. "You know something? You kids gonna drive me crazy."

She studied her sandaled feet. There was a smudge of manure on her big toe. She tried balancing on one foot and crooking her ankle enough so that she could rub the offending toe on the grass.

After he saw she was not going to answer him, Muhner said, "Ahh, why not. Why should I care?"

She gave him half the puffballs to seal the contract.

It meant doing without the pump for a while at least, until Jeff could get taken on for a few more days' work at the sawmill. The weather was still mild. She pointed out, reasonably enough, that it was she who hauled the water anyhow. He was the hewer of wood, she the drawer of water.

"You realize what you're doing, Robinowitz. It's all very symbolic. You refuse to marry me, but you're buying our child. You're buying us a goddam four-legged child, that's what you're doing."

The little fawn-colored calf trembled when they took him out of his wooden crib. She named him New Jersey. Muhner fashioned a rope halter for him. Muhner donated a lead line and a dented pail and New Jersey left his destiny behind and came to live with them in the woods.

Days, Robin staked him in the choicest grassy patches. He slavered green scum in the pail, but soon learned to sip water, cattle-fashion. Nights, she penned him in the lean-to that had sheltered their supplies before the house went up. Every morning she brushed and polished him till his hide shone like watered silk. And every twilight she forked his droppings into the wheelbarrow and lugged the collection over to Muhner's manure heap.

A week later the knacker came and backed his truck against the ramp. One by one the vealers, squealing, prodded to extremes, were loaded. Robin took New Jersey for a long walk in the other direction. He browsed. Wisps of green stalks stuck out of his mouth at a rakish angle. She picked wild sorrel and an armful of black-eyed Susans. One thing she had down to perfection: how to walk away from bad endings.

Fall was exceptionally mild that year. The trees held their leaves, the tomato plants continued to send up new green fruit.

And the garden stayed. They were still picking sweet corn when the college semester began.

After class, Robin took some to Tante, who stripped the kernels from the cob with a wicked-looking knife. She had lived more than fifty years in this country, but still frowned on eating corn American-style.

"Delicious, Binnie. And this late in the year. But you can't prolong your . . . estivation indefinitely."

"I like it. I may stay all winter."

"But your appointment. How will you meet your classes?"

"It's not as though I were a professor, Tante. I only have two sections twice a week."

"Back and forth on the highways in all weathers? Twice a week in that disreputable van?"

"It has brand new snow tires."

"Now, Binnie, I know I'm not on the committee, but I must tell you that your grandmother is very worried about you."

"She likes to worry. It keeps her weight down."

"Your grandmother expects to be molested on every street corner, so you can imagine what she thinks of your driving over those country roads alone in the dark."

"It's all superhighway. Door to door, only an hour and twenty minutes."

"Your grandmother sees you driving with a hitchhiker's gun at your temple." She made a little *moue.*

It was an intricate gavotte. They had always moved to the music this way, the two old women who cordially disliked each other, yet cherished the same child. Robin had memorized all the steps.

"I have a calf now," Robin said, and explained as simply as possible while leaving Jeff out. One could confess to loving animals. Loving animals was barely acceptable.

"So you're still the rescuer. I remember you at eleven, bringing home one stray cat after another."

"God! How Gran hated them."

"Your grandmother is quite phobic on the subject. Somehow they always managed to be pregnant when you found them."

Robin remembered mostly the disappearing kittens. Carted off to Angell Memorial, she now supposed. Or vivisected.

"You don't want to be a milkmaid all your life, do you? You have a fine mind, Binnie. But I'm afraid you're incurably romantic."

"Disgusting, keeping a barnyard pet," Gran pronounced. She preferred to forget that her ancestors had farmed potatoes. As a young girl she had been required to tend the chickens. "Very irresponsible of you, Binnie. The winters are terrible in those exposed places. I hope Tante isn't encouraging this whim of yours."

"Far from it," Robin murmured, awaiting the upsurge of the dance.

"It would be just like her to decide it was quaint or charming." She fished out her brooch from its hiding place. "Some day this will be yours, you know. You must realize that your great-aunt is a very impractical person. After Davis died, she went through the little he left her, like that"—she snapped her spatula-fingers—"and now she has to support herself, demean herself, really, with those French lessons and German lessons and teaching English to Orientals."

"Poor thing," Robin obliged.

"Yes, poor thing. I'm very fond of her, Binnie, as you well know, but she is a foolish woman."

And you're another, Robinowitz, she said to herself driving

home. To build is to dwell. It was the night of the first hard frost. The pasture grass was spangled with frozen dew and the roof of New Jersey's lean-to was bearded with white. In the house the wood stove popped its cheeks.

Jeff made cocoa. "How'd it go?"

She held the mug in both hands, considering. "Well, they didn't rend their garments or tear their hair, if that's what you mean."

"You didn't tell them."

"I told them about New Jersey."

"That's about what I thought you'd do, Robinowitz. Why are you holding out on them? Wasn't I on the list? 'Take Tante corn.' 'Order New Jersey's hay.' Why didn't it say, 'Tell about Jeffrey Rabinowitz?' You skin your hair back in a knot like a schoolmarm, you sharpen all your pencils, you make all those lists. Lately I've been noticing. I think you write things down just so you can cross them out."

"Then you're lucky I didn't write you down."

"No, dammit, you don't write me down. You're living with me, you fuck with me but you don't even write me down."

"For God's sake, Jeff! Two old ladies, they're living in another world. 'Someday all this will be yours, Binnie.' What do you want me to do?"

"Tell them."

"They were all the mother I ever had. Don't you want me to respect *their* world?"

"I want you to respect *mine.*"

"Well, what the hell am I doing here if I don't respect it?" She slammed down the mug so that some cocoa leapt the rim. "Chasing back and forth to the city. Bringing in a paycheck so you can have a year free to write in."

He pushed back his chair. "If I tell you what you're doing here you won't like it."

She was equally grim. "Then don't tell me."

But in bed they repaired the quarrel. It was something they could do together.

❋ NEW JERSEY WAS FRISKY but tame as a back-yard pony. Once the garden was down, Robin let him roam. He browsed among the corn stalks but there was nothing left to trample. He had a favorite scratching tree where the bark had been abraded by his hypnotic scrubbing motions, and a dusty place on the path behind the barn for rolling. Often he stood for hours with his nose on the window ledge, his liquid eyes with the now-darkening irises following Robin about the house.

Near the end of October New Jersey kicked out the side of the shed during the night and wandered off in answer to some elusive longing. They tracked him all morning in a steady rain. The weather had turned sharp. Leaves fell in freshets, whipped along by the wind. The click and thump of acorns and hickory nuts dropping imitated the sound of the calf's hoofs on stone. At noon they heard him lowing.

He had tried to leap over a stone wall that stood now in deep woods where once a pasture had been. A strand of barbed wire had raked him along the left flank and circling in his frenzy to free himself he had hopelessly tangled one foot. Jeff stamped back to borrow Muhner's wire cutters. Robin huddled in the rain with the enraged calf.

From then on, she kept him tied. Although he was docile enough with her still, the little buds on his forehead were sprouting into amber-colored horns. Dogs infuriated him. Displeased, he would lower his head and charge. Jeff, leading him to or from the shed, now carried a switch.

It snowed in time for Christmas. Robin gave Jeff a pair of boots, a Flexible Flyer, and a new translation of Heidegger's *Poetry, Language, Thought.* It asked, "What is it to dwell?" And answered; "Dwelling is the manner in which mortals are on earth." A red winter sunset was staining the tops of the oak trees, which alone husbanded their leaves, clay-colored, now shot with purple. New Jersey wore on his halter the silver package ribbon from Robin's new bathrobe, a gift from Gran. The little bull's fur was thick and newly fuzzy, and when he snorted he sent two jets of white steam into the air. They took him with them sledding in the back pasture. Currier and Ives had not thought of it.

Jeff gave Robin a bathtub. It wasn't a surprise (he had spent all week installing the hot water heater), but a luxury. While she soaked he read to her from Heidegger. "Earth is the serving bearer, blossoming and fruiting, spreading out in rock and water, rising up into plant and animal."

One thing marred the day. She had not visited the old ladies. She still had not put "Tell about Jeff Rabinowitz" on the list.

In January the air grew suddenly lax. For a week melting snow puddled the barnyard, the roads, the hollows between trees. Robin wedged a beach chair in the sinking snow and sunbathed, daydreaming when she should have been grading themes. Jeff, inside, pecked away at the typewriter, an essay on bridges that conduct man leisurely or in haste from here to there, there to here. The symbol is inherent, is not merely pasted on afterward.

The freeze came that night, with an ice storm. Driving was not simply treacherous, as the radio admonished, but impossible. Everywhere the puddles had become frozen lakes. New Jersey could not be taken out of his shed. The wind, coming across the Mink Hills, brought down ice-weighted branches and scoured the snow crust to a tight, upholstered surface. Staying warm required a constant vigil. Downdrafts scattered burning nuggets out of the fireplace and from time to time the wood stove sent clouds of smoke into the room.

The confinement at first was an adventure. Then annoying, then corrosive. Robin baked bread. There was time for kneading and for rising. She outlined a course in the American short story. She set about choosing fiction to illustrate contemporary theories about the family, community, work ethic, religion, race. Jeff finished his bridges essay and began on time, space, and distance. The relation between nearness and short interval. Attitudes toward the remote. Vanishing points.

By the second day he was out of tobacco and sucked on an empty pipe, which irritated her.

On the fourth day she had a ridiculous desire to eat in a fancy restaurant. She put on a dress and tried a new way of fixing her hair.

Jeff came back from the shed to report that New Jersey was lame. "Where do you think you're going?"

"No place."

"Just playing dress-up?"

"Cabin fever," she said curtly and changed back to jeans.

"Likely it's just stiff from standing," Muhner said, feeling the leg. "Whoa there! Makes him mean, too, cooped up like this."

It warmed up enough in February to snow. Bountiful flakes, a fall of a foot overnight. A few days' respite, just long enough to get the roads open, and another storm. Driving toward town to pick up the highway was like slipping through a dazzling white tunnel. The road was packed and firm under the tires. Still, she had no sensation that the wheels turned. Daylight was only a little thing wedged between the dark spaces. It was Ethan Frome country.

"Imagine calling it the *spring* semester," she said. They were cutting wood. So many dead birches had come down, and birch made a quick fire. It was her job to feed the tree along the trough of the big wooden cradle to his waiting chainsaw, then stack the logs while he positioned a new tree.

"It'll *be* spring, Robinowitz. It's part of the purposeful system."

" 'And since to look at things in bloom,' " she said. "Things in bloom! Wait a minute, will you?" She pulled off her mittens and chafed her red hands.

"Cold?"

"No. They itch."

"Chilblains."

"Chilblains belong in Dickens," she said. Nevertheless, she went inside.

That was the afternoon New Jersey gored Muhner's dog.

Robin had taken the bull out for a little trot, just long enough to get the blood moving was the way she thought of it. He was a solid, determined animal now, blond, handsome, with a long loose gait. Jeff was stacking the last of the wood, snug and neat as a Christmas card, against the house. It was a new dog, a collie pup left to its own resources. When it worried his heels, New Jersey broke away, wrenching her arm. The lead line flapped. He tossed the dog on his horns as if it were a ball of clay.

Blood stained the snow. The windows of Muhner's house were blank. He had gone to visit a cousin in Weare.

She waited up till midnight, watching the road for his car. She

didn't sleep. A pair of ghost horns came and went in the doorway of her mind.

"He's got to go," Muhner said in the morning. The dog's
carcass lay on a burlap sack. It was impossible to bury it.

"Is there anything we can do? I'd like to pay you for . . ." what
were the words? The murder? The accident? "For what happened."

"You got to sell that bull," Muhner said. "I told you, Robin.
Way back last summer, Robin. I told you, a calf is one thing,
a bull is dangerous."

She tried to remember if he had ever called her by name
before.

"Yes," she said.

"It's only nature," he said. "A bull now, the older he gets.
You know? He's only thinking one thing. That's what makes
him so mean."

"Yes," she said. If it were Jeff she would have put her hands
over her ears.

"You want me to ask for you? I can call the dealer."

She said "Yes" once more and walked back slowly to the little
house. It was funny how everything came so sharply into focus.
All the whiteness, all the reaching arms of the trees. The curl
of chimney smoke that had once said *to build is to dwell.* A
house of weathered, mismatched boards. No better than a squat-
ter's shack.

"What did he say?"

"Nothing."

"Come on, Robinowitz. He must have said *something.*"

"He said it was all right, okay?"

"All *right?* Didn't you offer to pay him something?"

"Of course I did! You knew I was going to."

"And what did he say?"

"He called me Robin," Robin said.

❋ JEFF HAD A CHANCE to work on the road crew. Twenty-five dollars a day, salting and sanding. She did not teach again till Thursday; she waved him off in the bus.

Around noon Muhner knocked. It sounded clumsy, that rapping, where nothing was fastened.

"He'll come tomorrow," he said. "Eighteen cents a pound is all. It isn't much, considering the care you gave him."

"It's fair," she said.

"Naw, it oughta be twenty, twenty-two at least." Muhner looked uncomfortable. "But it's the wrong season, see, and he's got to bring his truck over the road."

"Don't tell me! Just don't tell me about it."

❋ SHE PUT ON her dress-up dress. She packed nothing. She wanted nothing from this time of housebuilding and keeping. She took only an armload of books and this week's themes.

Muhner drove her to the bus stop in his snowplow jeep.

"Man is a combination of chance events," she told her reflection in the blue-tinted window. "From the biological point of view there is nothing unique about him." A false summer sky smiled back at her over the white landscape. *This goes double for animals. And triple for you, New Jersey.*

2

A Taste of Happiness

A EUPHORIC WIND across Boston Harbor blew on Robin Parks's great-aunt between glaucoma operations. In Zurich it is said that the raw wind out of the north causes children to quarrel, lovers to become impotent, wives to give way to melancholia, and the harried heads of families to take their own lives. In Boston, metaphysics are not thought to attend an onshore breeze. Nevertheless, it was Axel Gaul Laurent who brought the winds of change to Tante.

He was a small, collected man, neat just this side of finickiness. On introduction, he grazed the knuckles of Robin's right hand with his dry lips. If it had not been for their warmth she might have been caressed, she thought, by doeskin. Almost her great-aunt's age, he walked with none of Tante's hesitation. Except for a slight stoop to his shoulders, except for the little vertical lines that had begun now to crosshatch the horizontal creases on his forehead, and the smile wings at his eyes, he might have been taken for a man of sixty. His gray hair was still striped with blond lashings and waved along the back of his collar, and his mustache was full, running out above the edges of his mouth as symmetrically as an ant hill. His vision was perfect.

Tante had suffered always from poor eyesight, a weakness cheerfully attributed to the habits of her childhood. Her feckless stepfather had ventured from Paris to Berlin, Berlin to Zurich to Rome, and the child had been packed along as simply as an extra trunk. "Books, books, my only true friends," she said often to Robin. "I looked awful, Binnie. They dressed me like Sarah Crewe, but I put my nose in a book and read far beyond my years. Goethe, Heine, Schiller. The French classics, of course, those scandalous confessions of Rousseau. Balzac and Zola, from start to finish." And Robin could see the little scarecrow child reading away in *wagon-lits,* under the eiderdown in cold hotels, at table during the one-pot suppers in boarding houses. "Oh, I put my eyes out far too young," Tante said, but added with satisfaction, "of course always in the original. It enhanced my vocabulary."

She carried a cane. It seemed to Robin that she had always carried a cane for flourishes and thumps. "I have absolutely no depth perception," she told Axel the way other women might confess, I have absolutely no will power when it comes to chocolates. And she read still omnivorously, horripilated by modern fiction, yet determined to keep abreast. When the weather was favorable, she carried her book to the Boston Common and sat with her back to the State House and followed the dancing print with a see-through ruler. Caught in that moment of absorption, she had the earnest face and long jaw of an obedient pony. Her mouth sulked somewhat in repose; she set it straight whenever she thought of it.

Childlessness, she believed, draws down the most willing lips, and childlessness was her one public sorrow. In all the years of their marriage, Davis, now long buried, had never reproached her for it. It was not a question of fault—his spotty sperm? her unwilling ovaries?—but of destiny. And Binnie was like a daughter, just as her mother had been before her. But life was not art. Art was literature, a transport, a journey of the mind while the ruler set a straight path to guide by. And yet, modern novels depressed her. "A good romance ought to begin with earthly bliss," she said to Robin. "In opera at least one knows what to expect. And the Greeks. They understood how it was done, how fate deals the blows."

The book was *Couples.*

"But it's all a religious allegory," Robin said, from the vantage point of Instructor in English part-time, at Bay Community College.

"Nonsense. Blake may be on the cover, but there are nothing but genitals in between." And then, later, "Tell me, Binnie. Is that what is meant by fellatio?"

There had been that sudden onslaught of pain in the night, a pain, she liked to say later, that surpasseth memory. There were the slow months during which her shaved eyelashes grew back, brittle wispy straws with sharp edges that surprised her exploring forefinger. There were the weekly visits to Dr. Wendler, who performed nasty little pressure tests, with her hurled backward in the chair to be assaulted by the machine that humped down from the ceiling. He would have to repair the other eye as well. Surgery in three to six months, when she was quite herself again, and this time, he assured her, with no sense of haste. Time to prepare, he advised.

At seventy-six, she told him, she needed very little preparation. After all, she was not so vain as to buy negligees and kimonos. There was not a single dinner party for her to cancel.

But there was Axel. He came faithfully to her apartment on Beacon Hill each Monday, Wednesday, and Friday at nine for his English lessons. She took his chesterfield with its slightly shabby velvet lapels, she poured out tea, and they sat at either end of the sway-backed sofa under the crowded bookshelves and diligently constructed their dialogues. Axel, in search of a word, nervously shot his cuffs. His cordovan leather shoes shone. The porcelain cup and saucer rode in his left hand as easily as a sailboat at its moorings.

For twelve years now, since Davis died and left her in ever more modest straits, Tante had augmented her income by giving language lessons. To failing high-school and college students she taught a remedial French and German, spiced with cookies, lozenges, and pleasantries. To incoming Orientals, many of them residents in Boston hospitals, she taught basic English. She undid their l's and replaced them with r's and was invited to authentic Korean or Thai dinners in back-street restaurants she had not known existed. She taught instinctively and stubbornly and boasted that she had never had a dropout.

Axel was Alsatian, heir to a title he preferred to disclaim. "He was born between the lines, so to speak," Tante said to Robin. "As a result, his French is impure and his German somewhat tainted. But how he avoided learning English I will never"— here Tante hesitated—"understand." Robin heard the suppressed phrase as simply as if it had been spoken. *To my dying day* had always invaded Tante's statements as regularly as a radio time signal, the spirited cliché of an old lady in charge of the inevitability of her own death. Now with the advent of Axel she was newly vulnerable. Let there be war, genocide, wanton killing. Let the scythe cut its swath. And let her sentence be postponed.

What did Axel do? She had the impression that he had once been in imports and exports, *objets d'art*. Although he had

officially retired years ago, he dabbled still. From time to time
they went to art auctions together, Tante in the girlishly flapping
pleated skirts she favored, and the ends of her immense scarf
trailing below her wrists like extra appendages. Axel wore always a small diamond stickpin. His collars were generously
starched. Occasionally a frayed thread emerged from the matrix
and stood up against his Adam's apple. He had a habit of
running his finger along the edge of the collar as if to forestall
any further unraveling. Whenever he bid on an article—a Shef-
field candelabrum, an ormolu platter—he did so with the
merest knowledgeable nod of his head or with a small gesture
of one hand. And when he dropped out of the bidding—the item
was overpriced, or a clever reproduction or somehow flawed—
his face simply grew somewhat more composed. He sat back
deeper in his chair and in himself. He had declared his maleness.
To bid was not to buy.

The courtship was sedate and took place by daylight. There
were small boxes of marzipan. There were the slightly drooping
flowers that are proffered by hawkers at subway kiosks. After
the English lesson they lunched together in a modest but au-
thentically French restaurant, alternately choosing crêpes or an
omelet, and when the check came Axel half turned from Tante
to unfold his cumbersome, European-style wallet. On Sundays
at the Gardner Museum there were musicales. In good weather
there was always the Public Gardens for a stroll, a chat, and
finally the holding of hands.

They rarely saw each other in the evenings. Tante did not
trust her cane after dark. On Fridays she dined regularly with
her sister-in-law, Robin's grandmother, in the solemn brownstone on Marlborough Street. Gran sent the cab promptly at six;
Gran ordered its return on the stroke of ten. Nothing had

changed in those fine-spun orange evenings, except for a certain diffidence toward the future. Tante had been given to a kind of roguish endurance: I would like to see the Gaspé in autumn once more before I die, she would say. Or, Next summer, if I live, I mean to go back to Paris by hook or by crook. Two small but definitive thumps of the cane, rather like the wagging of a dog's tail. Now it was as if a small voice, ever present, never vocalized, murmured inside her: *live now, live now.* Not a stoicism, nor a propitiating act. "Life is routinely fatal," she said to Robin. "It's greedy of me, Binnie, at my age, but I want more."

❋ FOR A LONG TIME, Axel eluded Gran. Tante took care that her two worlds did not overlap. Friday nights at the head of the table her sister-in-law, who had been widowed early and comfortably, sat straight and ribbed as a celery stalk. The backs of her hands ran now to liver spots and her hair was blue white. Her life had been a succession of dinner parties, of *pâtés* and cheese puffs served in the living room where crystal decanters glittered on the bar; of Irish serving girls in pale green uniforms from Filenes moving like twin soldiers down opposite lengths of the dining table. Between galas she attended the shops. Her fine hawk's nose, incurably British by descent, was in windy weather often beaded with one drop of her body's juices. The salesladies in all the specialty houses of the Back Bay knew her. Shoes here, in this little boutique behind its awning. Scarves there, just beyond the stone lion. Jacques for furs, Best & Co. for the blouses with Peter Pan collars she once bought for Binnie; Best & Co., now defunct. Peck & Peck a poor substitute. The galleries and art shops the length of Newbury Street favored her. She would not set foot in Bonwit Teller. She remembered when it

had been the Museum of Natural History and continued to
cherish a grudge against the desecration of that landmark.

Destiny, for the most part, obeyed her. She had long controlled the curvature of the earth, the weekly winding of the
ancestral clock in the hallway, the invitation list of two annual
philanthropic balls and the dispensation of small favors to distant relatives. She was not a stupid woman but the long habits
of narcissism had made her petty. She planned her life as carefully as a military campaign; every act she performed was predi-
cated on appearances. There were, after all, standards to be
adhered to. Born before the telephone, the radio, the Stanley
Steamer, she had fed the chickens on the family farm in Maine.
She had dirtied her shoes on the midway of country carnivals,
she had stood beside her grandfather, the editor of the Bridgton
Weekly, while the paper was put to bed, and at nineteen became
by marriage one of the Boston Lathams. Forty years a patron
of the Boston Symphony, she pretended to a musical knowledge
that eluded her, but actually could not tell Mozart from
Brahms, nor one operatic aria from another. At theater she sat
in the fifth-row orchestra on opening night. Presuming on a
once-brief acquaintance, she always went backstage, for instance, to see Kit Cornell. Her hold on herself was firm but
precarious. Whenever she reported a conversation or an event,
she replayed it so that the other party—doorman or doctor,
soloist or shopgirl—addressed her by name. Mrs. Latham, he
said, she said, they all said. My dear Mrs. Latham. Lydia Latham was not to be trifled with.

Whereas Tante, more or less demure in captivity, was capable
of certain deceptions. "You must promise me, Binnie. Not a
word to your grandmother. *Pas un mot.*"

Tante, wearing her sunglasses although there was no sun,

fixed those two green moons on Robin's face. The old woman's skin, on which she had scorned to lavish creams and lotions, had a crisp and papery sheen as if subject to rents and three-cornered tears. Unlike Gran's, fed fifty years with turtle oils and emollients. Tante had married late, the lesser brother; Gran, headstrong and early, the winner. Between them lay the necessary vendetta, as simple as a good appetite, taking the place of love.

And Robin, who rode between the two old ladies as a courier might bear messages between opposing fiefdoms, pledged her silence. She told only Jeff, who remained pinned up in her mind, although she had left him in a bad time and without stating her reasons, which were anguished but unformulatable. He had not let her cut him off, after all. He wrote, he called; and finally she wrote, she answered. It was in abeyance, not over. And then he materialized in her little office at the college overlooking the harbor. Outside, the wrecker's ball, bringing down a row of outworn warehouses to make room for the expanding school, made a comfortably steady thud, raising dust and fumes across the view. Jeff, who was not on the list of charity balls, his existence unknown to Gran, whose table he had never graced. Jeff was a presence tacitly acknowledged to Tante. Because Tante loved a secret. Tante conspired and cherished.

"Why not?" he said. "We could all get married together. They could stand up for us, and we could stand up for them."

Robin saw a dusty parlor with bric-a-brac on the mantelpiece and a great gray fern breathing by the window. The wife of the justice of the peace wearing red felt slippers. She shook her head to clear the vision.

"Well, why shouldn't they, for God's sake? Just because you won't marry *me*, Robinowitz. If you can't make music, do you go around busting fiddles?"

"It just doesn't seem right."

" 'Judge not' and all that. It doesn't have to seem right."

"Do you suppose they sleep together?"

"So that's what bugging you. Seeing your mother figure in that Biblical act of fornication."

"But it's so ridiculous! They're too old for those acrobatics."

"It's the last thing that dies," he told her. "Maybe they do and maybe they don't. It's nobody's business, anyway."

"All that sagging flesh," she said. "Gran will have a fit. An absolute fit."

"Why?"

"Why? I'll tell you why. She'll say it's unseemly at their age."

"Bullshit, Robinowitz. Since when is it seemly to be lonely? Your grandmother's jealous. Besides, she's losing power. It'll be one more defection from her little kingdom."

But not me, Robin said to herself. *Not me, I haven't defected.*

❊ "IT'S VERY cowardly of you, Tessa," Gran said. "Cowardly to tell me in Binnie's presence, knowing that she would defend you. Knowing full well the strength of my objection."

Dinner had gone down smoothly enough. The lobster bisque was of the palest coral tint and properly laced with Madeira. Crab cakes, because, as Gran had said with the steel of triumph in her morning voice, "Heaven knows, she can't afford them elsewhere, Binnie. And I don't invite my relatives to pot roast." But knowledge of the coming ordeal had dried out the patties in Robin's mouth. She could not remember tasting anything she had chewed.

"Utterly ridiculous at your age, Tessa. With your failing eyesight, and another serious operation confronting you." Robin waited for *unseemly.* It did not come. "And what do you know about this man? His background, his resources? You'd be better off with a guide dog! Stomping around Zurich with your cane. All those Alps, and you in totally unfamiliar surroundings. It's unthinkable, Tessa. It's . . ."

"*Dégoutant,*" Tante murmured.

"And don't you dare lapse into French in my house. I won't stand for it. Half-blind or not, you could at least remember your manners. Now what did you say?"

"I said, my dear Lydia," Tante said clearly, "I don't need my eyesight to marry."

❋ THE CEREMONY took place, as Robin had expected it would, in the front room on Marlborough Street. There were flowers massed on the grand piano, flanking a picture of Davis, exhumed from the attic and splendid in a silver frame. Gran's one public spite, it was mitigated by the champagne and five kinds of hors d'oeuvres that were borne alongside. Judge Ardmoor of the Third District Court had been persuaded to perform the ritual, and seventeen people—including several former students of Tante's—were present. Jeffrey Rabinowitz was one of them, although Robin had not put him on the list. Tante passed him off—black beard, curly shoulder-length hair—as a "dear friend and ally," and Axel embraced him in the Gallic tradition with a buss on either cheek.

Afterward Gran remarked, "Given the extraordinary number of foreigners, Binnie, I think we did well to bring it off in English at all, don't you?"

"But they all speak English," Robin protested.

"More or less. The best of the batch was that rabbinical student of hers, didn't you think? Not a trace of an accent, at least from what one could hear through the beard."

"That was my lover," Robin murmured into a Fuji chrysanthemum.

"What did you say, Binnie? I can't bear it when you mutter those stagey asides."

"I was agreeing with you, Gran. He was the best of the batch."

The art of capitulation is grace. Gran had acceded not only with Mumms and imported caviar, but lavished upon Tante at the moment of departure two gifts. One was a diamond bracelet from Shreve, Crump and Low. It glittered in the jeweler's box like a newborn snake. The other, an antique ring of four winking emeralds, slid dramatically from her own finger to be thrust over her sister-in-law's knobbed joint. It was a ring that Gran had always disdained despite its market value, complaining that it was as gaudy as a Christmas-tree bauble. But the gesture was a calculated one. Robin had been sent earlier that week to have one wobbling gem reset.

Nevertheless, the stalwart old ladies stood in the airport walkway and were linked by that awkward clasping, and two surprised tears oiled Tante's cheeks.

Axel, who called her always "dear lady," received Gran's frosty best wishes. Although she disapproved of the custom, she permitted him to kiss her hand. After which the shyly attentive bridegroom drew his bride's arm through his own and the couple emplaned for Zurich.

❀ ROBIN'S OFFICE at the college, now that the warehouses had been demolished, admitted full afternoon sun. Tante's little avocado plant, given into her safekeeping, sat in the pool of light hazed over with dust motes. The stem bobbed mutely back and forth in the draft. Not a leaf had fallen, nor had a new one sprouted in the ten days since Tante had gone.

On the day that she returned, unexpected, alone, it put up a new mint-green tip.

Robin carried it back to Tante's apartment the next afternoon. Pluck is what is called for in the face of adversity. Pluck is a starchiness that does not give way to self-pity. When the bridegroom absconds at dawn from the Zurich Excelsior with an heirloom ring, with a bracelet of numerous brilliants and five hundred dollars in newly cashed travelers' checks, pluck is a rising above the shattered dream.

There was no reason, then, not to get on with the operation. Dr. Wendler, his full mouth murmurous at her temples, had measured her intraocular pressure for the last time. He pronounced her ripe.

The night before surgery in Tante's room at the hospital, she spoke of the marriage for the first time. Her hair, loosed from its bun, had been braided in two thin plaits that fell on either side of the pillow. The pale bony face, the bleached linen, the ribbed counterpane were all a study in whiteness. Without ornament or talisman Tante lay in the reduction of her body, a docile animal.

Gran had earlier delivered herself of her outraged feelings; Tante had not flinched. One quaint phrase from that tirade lingered.

"Horse-and-buggy ride, indeed," Tante said after she had gone. "What does she know? She grew up on a chicken farm. It wasn't a horse-and-buggy ride at all. More a *folie à deux.*"

"Don't be sorry," Robin said, fiercely sorry that instant for everyone but reserving the best regrets for herself, the captive listener.

"I dreamed there was this city," Tante said. "It was small like a doll house and in the dream I was totally blind, I had to feel my way past little lampposts, little cars, buildings with door-knobs. There was the bell pull from the concièrge's apartment in Paris, and the Tower of London and Westminster Bridge, very fragile, made out of matchsticks. And snow, it was real snow, I remember, I held some in my hand while it melted."

"So it was a toy marriage," Robin said, mortified for herself, the leftover daughter with visitation rights.

"No, it was real, I remember the dream. The little cafés with paper umbrellas, the tables and chairs as big as my thumb. I wish it had never happened."

"Oh, Tante! Remember the good parts. There were some good parts, weren't there?"

"I gave of myself unstintingly. I brought him his English. His moods and conjugations. But I wish it had never happened."

Robin begged, "But you were happy."

"It isn't the scandal, Binnie. At my age it is hard to scandalize anyone. It isn't the financial loss or the complications of it all. No, it's because a taste of happiness is hard to bear."

* 3 *

The Primal Scene

ONCE OR TWICE a year, though never over a holiday when people were convivial and there was ice in the silver bucket and bottles on the bar, Robin's mother came home. Back from the san—they always called them sans—for a trial visit. Sometimes, after a week, she re-entered the same san. More often she carried on shrilly for half a day, declaiming, "I won't go back! I refuse to go back to that miserable hole!" At forty-six she was slim and small-boned and favored the exaggerated gestures of a young woman, as if rehearsed before a mirror. Afterward a flurry of consultations and phone calls would ensue and Gran would then initiate, wearily, a new plan.

"I've just heard of the most marvelous place, Beth. Very small, only twenty carefully selected residents, and it's quite close by, in the Berkshires." Or the Adirondacks, or the White Mountains, as if an institution for wealthy alcoholics and psychoneurotics required the crags and peaks of a t.b. cure. "You'll love it there, Beth, it's full of creative people, artists and musicians. There's a studio for sculpting and they have their own chamber-music group." Gran, a puffier version of her daughter, imperious in all other matters, smoothing the way in this one.

Robin had not wholly counted on the way her mother's eyes had exploded in some inner disaster this time, so that little rods of navy blue danced and wavered on the paler sea of her irises. She thought of the safety of brown eyes, wet and furry and impenetrable (Jeff's). But the eyes of her parent who was almost a stranger shifted, far to near, near-far, and were tinged with pink at the edges. Two bright capillaries, shifty as worms, moved as the eyes moved their focus.

Gloria came within them. Gloria, her nurse on loan from the san, moved on rubber suction soles that squeegeed as she walked. She had a bobbing stride, feet placed apart as though her inner thighs were gluey and contrived not to touch. Gloria had crippled hair of a harsh metal color that had been razored in layers for a gamin effect.

When her mother came home, Robin took the back room on the second floor. It had once been a sleeping porch. Now all the leavings of her girlhood, and of her mother's before her, were stored there. The brown varnished window casings had crazed and the panes, lacking putty, rattled in the slightest wind. She heard the two of them overhead in the third-floor rooms all curtained in white that Gloria referred to as "your mother's apartment." Gran said it, too, but drily. "Are you going up to your mother's apartment for tea? Then take this to Miss Barnum." "Miss Barnum," Gran persisted in calling her at dinner, which they all took together, uneasy as new boarders. "Miss Barnum's gone away, Gloria's here," she answered sweetly.

Upstairs, continually, the rattle of closet doors, the rhythm of a rocking chair, the sounds of the living. A murmur and cooing cry. Against the snap of a shade being sent up and the counterpoint of two voices, Robin remembered her father. The few things she could call back about him had gotten paler and thinner. He was a tall cardboard figure in a popout book whose wide smile uncovered perfectly pearly teeth, rather beaverlike in front. Her nose in his neck sniffed up a ripe male smell as strong as bitten apple and overlaid with tobacco. She did not remember him in the uniform of an Army captain, or before that, in his doctor's coat. She was four years old when he died by mistake in an American air strike just before the Korean truce. Of his clothes she remembered best the bow ties, polka dots and stripes, that puffed at an angle under his collar, and a way her mother then had of fingering his lapels as if to restore him to symmetry. She supposed she remembered that close gesture because it shut her out.

Early on, of course, Tante was invited to dinner. The second operation had produced only mediocre results. Dr. Wendler was snappish, disappointed in his patient and himself. The trouble was, Tante lacked humility. Accustomed to the genteel poverty of European intellectuals whom wars had displaced, she had no defensive residue. "I plan to keep my eyes and my bowels open as long as possible," she told Wendler. "This limited vision is a hard judgment to be passed on me. But after all, I am still very young in my dreams." Bareheaded in all weather, she twirled her cane for emphasis.

"You're far too thin," she accused Beth. "You don't get outdoors enough. And what do you think of our Binnie now, with her Master's degree and her teaching?"

But they were still very shy with each other, the mother and daughter. Beth's arm, squirrel-like and tremulous, darted to Robin's waist. "Wonderful," she said. She dared a little squeeze, then detached herself and stepped apart.

"And this is Miss Barnum," Robin said. "My great-aunt, Mrs. Latham."

"Oh, but you *must* call me Gloria."

"Gloria is my dearest friend," Beth said.

"Elle a une façon d'être qui est vraiment trop familière," Tante found occasion to murmur to Robin.

"It is extremely rude," Gran said, "to speak French in mixed company. That is a rotten habit of yours, Tessa. You do it all the time."

"You are absolutely right," Tante said peaceably. "Forgive me. I forgot myself."

Conversation was awkward. Tomato juice had replaced cocktails in the living room. There was no wine at dinner.

"We ought to begin doing things together," Gran said from the head of the table. Although everyone had been served, she fussed with the carving knife and tested the edge against her flat yellow thumb. Had it lost its bite? "For instance, Pops, now that the Symphony is over. And the van Gogh exhibit at the Museum this month. Perhaps we could have a few people in. Some friends of *yours,* Binnie."

"Won't you have some more salad, Gloria," Robin said to deflect attention from the friends she most passionately resisted inviting.

"You must never say 'more of' something," Gran began. "It calls attention to the fact that a person is having a second helping, and . . ."

"It's extremely rude," Robin and Beth finished in a chorus that surprised them both.

"I won't be mocked." Gran squared her back.

"Lydia, I'm sure it was a spontaneous . . . tribute to your upbringing," Tante put in.

Gran ignored her. "Please do have some salad, Miss Barnum."

For once, Gloria was cowed out of "Miss Barnum's gone away."

"Your daughter seems to have absolutely no friends." Gran addressed Beth, who focused on her plate. "No friends. I don't understand it. None she wants to confide to us, at any rate."

Robin muttered, "They're not on the list."

"What did you say, Binnie? Don't mumble."

There was a long silence which Robin refused to break. Gloria nervously served herself salad. The bowl clattered as she put it down.

"Bitch," Beth said finally into the hush, and kicked over a water glass with the heel of her hand. "You dowager bitch." She pushed away from the table.

"If you'll excuse me," Gloria said. "I think I'd better go with her."

"You'll do nothing of the kind," Gran said serenely. "We will not glorify a tantrum. Will you have some roast, Tessa?"

Nevertheless, Gloria went.

"Yes, thank you, I believe I will," Tante said, after the door had closed behind the nurse, and permitted her plate to be refilled.

Robin thought, But she has no pride! And then thought, No, she has no sense of embarrassment, that's her secret weapon. Tante nearsightedly attacked the meat. Robin chewed doggedly although her throat had closed and she had no hope of being able to swallow. She tried to think how Jeffrey Rabinowitz, who was pre-eminently not on the list, would have responded. *It sounds to me,* he said, as she pretended to tell him, *like an anxiety crisis. I mean, all her touchstones, all her criteria for testing, keep crumbling. It's a symbolic tribal thing, her matriarchy. So she has to demonstrate that she's still in charge. And then she provokes a palace revolution that she can't quite put down.* After which she not only swallowed the mouthful but forked up another.

Nevertheless, they did begin doing things together, the little army of five women. They went to the première of a comedy which Gran pronounced "a dreadful little French farce." "Not in the least à la mode," Tante countered. They perched on narrow-backed gilt chairs at the Gardner Museum while a young soprano sang a group of Schumann's Lieder. "A sweet enough voice, but too thin," was Gran's verdict. "Sometimes I think your grandmother is totally tone deaf," Tante said to Robin. Lulled by the color slides of a lush tropical landscape Gran fell asleep during a travelogue at New England Mutual Hall. "In spite of her experience," Tante commented, "she's very insular. She has a provincial disregard for the rest of the world."

Laughter overhead that night. Until very late, the rise and fall of voices in husky, coppery tones. What did they find to say to each other? *Gloria is my best friend.*

Robin wrote to Jeff, but did not plan to mail it.

Once you were my mother, Robin thought. Once you were my age and stuck pins in my diaper—the incongruity did not immediately occur to her—and heated the milk. She imagined how Beth had tested it on the delicate blue patch of her inner wrist. And then disloyally: even then you were drizzling sherry all day into an orange-juice glass. Tante had said it once as they curled on the faintly musty sofa in her apartment under the bookshelves heavy with the Victorians and sipped their raffish sweet cocktails. "Sometimes I blame myself, Binnie. We did the very same thing, your mother and I, from the time she was sixteen or so. Oh, she came here for refuge, she was a very lonely adolescent after all, growing up in that . . . mausoleum. But sometimes I think I encouraged that dreadful taint in her. Your Uncle Davis used to warn me. You must guard against it, Binnie."

"Don't worry, Tante. It's not something you inherit."

"You inherit brains, why not that . . ."

"Fatal tendency?" Robin finished. "I don't know. It's acquired, I think. You can't inherit a craving."

They went shopping one day, just Robin and Beth. Wary together, but arms linked as if to sustain the fragile ethic of mother and daughter. Down Marlborough Street the magnolias were just falling from bloom, a debris now where once white petals had opened their waxy mouths on a delicate frill of pink in their throats. The swan boats were running. Marigolds and zinnias, still holding back their buds, were up in the Gardens in lines like toy soldiers, and the peanut vendor was back. They dallied to feed the pigeons, unwilling, Robin thought, to violate the detailed fretwork of early summer by going indoors.

Beth said, "Tell me something. What Gran said the other night. About your friends."

"What about them?"

"Well, why aren't you living with them in a commune or something? Why are you pitching your tent between these two old ladies?"

"I could ask you the same thing," Robin said. "For instance, why did you come back?"

"I'm just drying out between sans, baby. Nothing is any different. Do you want to tell me?"

"I *was* living with somebody," Robin said. "Not a commune. Just the two of us."

"And?"

"And it didn't work out."

"Are you in love with him?"

"Right this minute, you mean? Or then?"

"Whichever you want," Beth said.

"I don't know. I'm just drying out between lovers."

"God," Beth said suddenly. "Here you are old enough to talk about lovers. God, I want a drink."

"You want some new clothes," Robin told her. "Anyway, wait for Gloria. You're not going to kick over the traces with me."

"Does it scare you?"

"Why should it? I'm used to it."

"Don't judge me, baby. That's all I ask. Good things are in store for you."

The phrase set up an echo. "From now on, it will happen to you every month," Gran had said, unwrapping the sanitary napkins. "It will happen, Binnie, and it will mean that you are a woman. Biologically. With all that implies." She looked uncomfortable. "Fortunately, all that is behind me."

It will never come again, Robin had promised herself fiercely. *I don't want it. I won't let it, not me, ever.* And hid the stained underpants in the bottom drawer of the Hepplewhite bureau and month after month flushed away the bloodied Kleenex and pretended she had won.

Until on the eve of her Latin final she took her datives and ablatives to Tante for unscrambling. "Menses, Binnie," Tante said firmly. "A good Latin word. Your grandmother is very worried about you. It seems that you don't wish to accept the fact. From time immemorial. Oh, I know! It's hard to come of age. In France we called it *mon ami.* Here I believe the euphemism is something odd, jumping off the roof."

"Falling," Robin whispered.

"Yes. Whatever. But you must learn to love your body, dear. It's not a guilty secret. Good things are in store for you."

And on this day in the Public Gardens, Robin took her mother's hand, smaller than her own. They went to Bonwit's and tried on a great many outfits and bought none of them.

Doing things together persisted. In a hard June rain the five women went to Members' Night at the Aquarium, a complicated arrangement requiring two taxis and multiple umbrellas. The wharf area was deserted. Rain drummed on the pilings with a melancholy sound and the wind whipped up a detergent-like foam against the pier. Pushing through the double doors into that huge clean-lighted space was like coming suddenly out of a sickroom on a scene of handsome children playing. It smelled like a cocktail party. People, holding their glasses aloft, touched and glided across the hall. The corridor enwrapped an enormous central glass tower of water through which various unusual fish swam. At the base of the tower a moat lit from below, with more fish, and a rock for pitching pennies. It was like a medieval fair.

"It's an ocean-going Guggenheim," Robin said. She successfully maneuvered Beth past the bar in the first-floor hallway and they started up the ramp.

Past the penguins. Past an array of sea robins, startlingly birdlike, and a tide-pool display with crabs.

Gloria stood at a window sequined with alewives, a thousand bright silver fingerlings in constant flux.

"They look so free."

"It's only another prison," Beth said. At the bottom of the tank a menhaden was attacking a dead or dying alewife—the rippling water made it impossible to tell which—and a little string of bright blood rose above the struggle to hang in the water like an exclamation mark. The little carnage took place without rousing the least interest among the rest of the school. Robin watched. How much of one fish could another of the same size digest? Most of it, was the answer. Sated, the menhaden twitched away, leaving the tail of the corpse. But when Robin moved on, Beth was no longer beside her. She had disappeared into the crowd.

Farther on there were eels, their electric impulses recorded as a magnified crackle. A tank of bass, another of ponderous sea turtles. At the top of the ramp, another bar beckoned, and beyond it, a glass in her hand, her mother stood on one foot contemplating an octopus.

Before Robin could get to her, Beth returned to the bar and held out her glass. Ice, and a tumblerful of what she guessed was vodka. Beth's head bobbed along the passageway, disappeared behind taller heads and reappeared, again fronting the octopus.

"So you got into it," Robin said when she reached her.

"So I did."

"Satisfied?"

"Mildly pleased, you might say. Look!"

The octopus streaked backward across the tank, trailing its tentacles like seaweed. At the other boundary the arms fanned out in rays across the glass. Each was dotted with suction cups which appeared to squeeze and release and take hold again in a languorous, individuated fashion.

"Not only can it hold on to anything," Beth said. "And I mean hold on. It can let go, like that. Marvelous control. Marvelous efficiency, don't you think?"

The octopus reached one arm into its mantle and fished out a clamshell. Discarded, the shell spiraled to the bottom and split apart as it settled. It was empty.

"It puts things in there in that sort of beak with one of its feelers." Beth pointed. "And then you see that sort of furry part of it moving up and down as if it were breathing? It's eating it, the clam or shrimp or whatever, it just sucks the goodness out. Then it reaches back in and takes out the bones." She explained it breathlessly, delighted. "They say they're very intelligent."

The octopus contorted its jellylike center, appearing to turn itself inside out. Robin saw the beak, wide as a fledgling bird's, and the stalks of eyes. It then began to crawl across the glass.

"It runs things wherever it goes," Beth said. She drank deeply. "The brain just squats there in the center and tells the rest of it what to do."

"It doesn't run everything," Robin said. "It got caught, didn't it?"

Beth turned wordlessly and stalked back to the bar.

Gloria caught up with them, finally. "Oh, God," she said. "How many of those have you had?"

"I don't know. Four or five."

"Give the glass to Robin right this minute or they'll see you. They'll see you and they'll send us back to the san."

"I'm perfectly sober."

"Well, you won't be if we don't get right out of here. *Please,* Beth. Please, my darling darling, put it down. I'll give you something better when we get home."

"A few lousy chlorals," Beth said darkly.

"No, something better," Gloria promised.

It was humiliating to listen to. It was cowardly to leave. The octopus detached itself in the same leisurely manner, then shot across the tank to the other wall.

"Try to behave yourself till we get home."

"I always behave myself," Beth said, spacing her words with elaborate care.

Overhead that night, neither murmur nor thump. No shifting of furniture, no prolonged running of water. Robin waited for the splash that signaled life walked overhead. Finally, uneasily she made her way up the familiar stairs in the dark house and listened at the door. The faintest susurrations. The crack of a light. She turned the knob.

They were naked. Gloria, golden and shining as if with oil, straddled the pale body of her mother sprawled loose as a Raggedy Ann doll on the bed.

"Oh, Robin. Oh, God, no." Beth groaned.

"It's not what you think," Gloria said, heaving herself to the floor. In the warm spill of light from the bedside lamp she rooted about for something to put on, but nothing had been flung down in haste.

"How could you," Robin said. And again, "How could you."

"Oh, my God, Robin," Beth kept saying. "Just what I didn't want. The one thing I didn't want."

Gloria meanwhile went to the closet and fetched out a bathrobe. She tied the sash in a double knot. Then she sat down at the foot of the bed and began putting on her shoes. White nurse's shoes with sensible faces. After she had concentrated for a long time on the laces, she faced Robin. "Some day," she said. "Some day you'll understand how it happens. In the sans that way, women living with women year after year."

Beth wept. "The one thing I ever asked. The one thing, don't judge me."

"It isn't that I really mind," Robin said finally. "It's just seeing it. I've only read about it."

Of this Jeff would have said, the primal scene. You know what the real primal scene is, don't you, Robinowitz? Not that unconscious memory of the parents coupling in the dark, that Norman O. Brown hang-up. It's not a dream you fall back into at all. No, the real primal scene is the first time you have to be a parent to your parent. The first time you have to be the forgiver.

✻ Part Two ✻

4

The Mary Jane Kitchen

T THE Washington's Birthday party the year before where
Robin first met Jeff, there were two kinds of music warring contrapuntally across the center hall. The Grateful Dead
were having at it in what had once been a formal dining room
heavily wainscoted in oak, and across the foyer behind the
French doors of the living room with its wide-fronted view of
the Hudson River, a Brandenburg concerto had just undertaken
its slow movement.

Standing alone at the bar in the crowded hall, Robin amused
herself for a long time by turning her head ever so slightly to
one side or the other to marry or sort out the discords. She was
drinking vodka and quinine water, but slowly because of the
bitter aftertaste. It was what her mother always drank when she
could promote a bottle between rest periods at Havenhurst or
Arden Acres or, this time, Payne Whitney, where Robin had
gone to see her earlier in the day. Totally sober, she was a tiny
woman, mild as a grasshopper. Robin brought her candy bars
and they made safe talk, like neighbors on adjoining porches.
For the swollen boiling creature she had been, with spittle rising
at the corners of her mouth and her vomit pooled on the carpet

like marmalade, determined the extent of the space between them. It was always there. A reason for sipping slowly, renouncing those genes.

Four individuals shared the expenses of this apartment—they could not be said to be living together—and one of them had been Robin's roommate in college.

"Y'all have to *meet* people," Sue Ellen said in a cross voice. The Southern collective was never to be cultured out of it. She twitched away in her tulip skirt and came back with her hand on the sleeve of Jeffrey Rabinowitz, tenant.

What Robin liked was the way his hair curled and ran down into his beard, as natural as pelt.

He freshened her drink and they shouted inanities at each other in the foyer as from opposite sides of a stadium.

"Let's get out of this rally," he called into her ear. "Which do you want, rock or Bach?"

"Bach, I think."

They settled by the living-room window overlooking the Hudson and made conversation with the caution of children who have been admonished in advance to like each other. The Spry sign, its back to the New Jersey shore, winked red and yellow. Traffic exhausts on the Drive below showed gauzy against the street lights, like cobwebs spun between toy trucks on a shelf. The city Frank Lloyd Wright had said they ought to tow out to sea on barges, all soundless and orderly eight stories down.

But what they talked about were kitchens they had known. His parents' seamless kitchen with a wall oven and gridless cooking top that confounded the maid. The brown-varnished kitchen at the back of her grandmother's house on Marlborough

Street where a series of important cooks had frowned and retied their aprons.

His own, idealized, would have a wood stove, its six burning eyes orange as an animal's at night. To one side, a pair of warming ovens. And six wooden cooking spoons would not be too many to hang above.

Moreover, his cupboards were open shelves where there would be no lurking. And from the rafters vegetables hung down as simply as shoelaces.

All this took place in his own house, which he would build with his own hands in the country.

In the kitchen that had been her lover's, the kitchen of a Finn with invisible eyelashes and pale, tufted hair, dill and coriander had grown in straw boxes hung around the window frame. The view faced a laundry and a delicatessen on Cambridge Street where the Harvard houses begin to melt into a shabbier working-class neighborhood. From time to time a roach would come awake on the drainboard when she flicked on the light at night. It was impossible, the landlord said, to eradicate them completely. Their headquarters lay far underground. Roaches had colonized the earth since the Flood, one had to be a good sport about them.

Toivo had roasted their Christmas goose overnight in an oiled paper bag. He had gotten up every two hours to sprinkle the brown paper with water. She did not speak of any of this.

From the pump that serviced Jeff's imaginary kitchen, spring water came forth in a series of hiccups; then, primed, poured out its natural good. Struck from rock as if by Moses. Nothing had been added to it.

While he talked, Robin suffered a confusion of kitchens,

vague ghosts from earliest childhood. A spattering of farmers on
the wallpaper of one, while her father was alive. Another, a
surgical chamber that dazzled with stainless steel and copper.
Twin spigots arched here like swans' necks and a silver bucket
sweated with ice. Later, she rode a tricycle in a room where
nothing was ever cooked and fruit rotted in the refrigerator until
it smelled like whiskey.

"You don't like my kitchen," he said.

The truth was she had not been listening. "I like the armchair
part and your feet up on a coal scuttle."

"You're a creative little liar, aren't you? What do you do in
your kitchen, Robin?"

"Bake bread." She was silent remembering.

"A bread maker. I know the type."

She crunched an ice cube. "I suppose you've been researching
the subject for years."

"No. I lived with one. My mother always made the challah
for Friday night."

"Rich women don't make bread."

"Jewish ones do."

"That's funny," Robin said. "Amy Goldstein's mother only
made the gefilte fish."

"Who the hell is Amy Goldstein?"

"No one I ever cared about. A girl at Radcliffe."

"Well, fuck Amy Goldstein. I bet you couldn't make bread
in our kitchen."

"Is it a Jewish kitchen?"

"No. It's a Mary Jane kitchen. Come on. I'll show you."

They started down the corridor but it was blocked with an
assortment of the curious.

"Will you keep the goddam door shut?" one of the hosts

pleaded. "Come on, Barry. You're wrecking the temperature."

It had once been a capacious linen closet. The walls and ceiling were lined with aluminum foil and fluorescent lights were rigged on a pulley. Two dozen marijuana plants now flourished where North Star blankets and monogrammed sheets had been stored. The greenery gave off a good garden smell, the July smell of a hayfield. Robin thought of tobacco sheds in Connecticut lined up like covered bridges.

"Kramer's cottage industry," Jeff said.

"But how does he dry it?"

"In the oven. On broil. He flash-cures the leaves."

She allowed herself to be threaded to his hand through the crowd, into the kitchen thick with the familiar herbal smell of pot. A sweet and ancient ritual was in progress. A sad-eyed boy sat on the stove and inhaled deeply, rolling his eyes as he dragged the smoke down and swallowed. Several others, draped on counters, shared a pair of joints. The sticks went around so fast that they overlapped where a pretty fat girl sat on the floor, her back against the refrigerator door. She brought both jays comically to her mouth, then switched hands and sent them back in opposite directions.

Sneezing, Robin followed Jeff. His room, two cubicles with a sink and toilet closeted in between, was where servants had lived.

"Irish girls, probably," he told her. "Right off the boat. Room and found and six dollars a week. My grandparents had an apartment a lot like this one; my mother grew up in this neighborhood. She used to roller skate on West End Avenue."

By now she was sneezing continually in little staccato bursts. Her eyes were running.

"What's come over you?"

"It's the pot," she apologized. "I'm allergic to it."

"Interesting. Did you have a bad trip once?"

"No. Just giant hives and this." She snuffled.

He got her some toilet paper.

"Don't tell me," he said while she blew. "You're also allergic to house dust, dog hair, cat fur, pollen and paint, shellfish, feathers, and perfume."

She shook her head. "Only marijuana and eggplant."

"Eggplant." It made him thoughtful.

On her twenty-first sneeze they left the apartment and went to a local pizzeria.

"Rate your childhood on a scale of one to ten," he said.

"One being the worst and ten the best?"

"Yes."

"Half," she said, after a brief hesitation.

"Half of what?"

"Half of one on the Richter scale of childhood happiness. Isn't that what you wanted?"

"One out of twenty? Five out of a hundred?"

She chewed, considering. "Out of a hundred, maybe two or three."

"That doesn't make any sense."

"It makes perfect sense to me. I can think of two or three times out of a hundred when I was completely happy. Once was riding a pony."

"I meant mathematically it doesn't make any sense."

"I thought you meant impressionistically."

"How can you measure things impressionistically?"

"You see?" she said, as if that settled it. "That's what's wrong with statistics."

"Robin. How do you bake bread, for instance, without statistics?"

"You mean, do I measure?"

"Yes."

She shook her head triumphantly. "I cook by motherwit."

"Did your mother teach you?"

"Not bloody likely." She tried not to embellish with too many of the sad details. Every time the door of the pizzeria opened, a fresh gust of wind laden with grit rattled through. It was like reading a book aloud and losing your place. Or she had had too much to drink. She hated the way people get confidential at midnight.

What he said was that if people didn't stay up past midnight eating pizza in their local greasy spoons they might otherwise turn to stone.

So then the matter of her grandmother, whom she lived with, and her great-aunt, who fluttered nearby, surfaced. Something of her sense of custodianship regarding them. The way they were her girls now, the way things get switched around.

"Imagine being sisters-in-law for fifty years," she said. "It's worse than sisters. All they have are their pasts and they lie about them all the time. My grandmother thinks that she's some sort of countess, making up lists for coming-out parties nobody goes to. Going up and down Bay State Road with her arthritis, insulting and firing specialists. She thinks she still matters! And Tante has pretended to be the poor lost relation so long that she believes it. She goes on and on about the poverty of her European childhood, living out of trunks, left behind in rooming houses, standing in the streets to see Isadora Duncan being pulled around in her carriage by students. All that rot. One of them has to be nobly born and the other has to be beholden. And all the audience is gone except for me."

He had had a brother named Dewey, two years older, a physicist and a schizophrenic, who killed himself at twenty-five. "He died while I was in Africa, goddam him," Jeff said. "In the middle of a chess game. His last move came posthumously. He had me, *en passant.*"

"That's so sad. When did he get sick?"

"I don't even know. I guess it was always there. He was always a sort of shaman. Until he was fifteen or so, he was just cocky and generous. A brash kid who was good at everything."

"And then all at once?"

"No. Imperceptibly, really. But if you knew him from the inside, you knew all along he had this murdering conscience. You knew that every shining thing he did he did to put down guilt."

"Guilt? For what?"

"Everything. Nothing. For getting good grades. For wearing his underwear two days in a row. Having a pimple. Jacking off in the john."

"You make him sound like an All-American boy."

"Well, finally he came apart, he couldn't speak or had terrible rages. Then there was the first shrink and the second, Dr. Spitzhoff. Sitzmark, we called him. He hated being in therapy. It was like he couldn't look at me any more."

Because of her mother she understood this.

"Then he committed himself. He'd burned up all his books one crazy afternoon and he couldn't stand the remorse."

She nodded. "And then it began to get worse?"

"Little by little. He killed himself gradually, a kind of suicide on the installment plan. In between, sometimes, he was perfectly lucid."

She couldn't say anything. Again she nodded to show that she knew.

"He came home one weekend and slit his wrists and wrote good-by in blood on the bathroom tiles. Later, I got this note. It came with the chess move, back in Africa."

"What did it say?"

" 'The steps of a man are ordered by the Lord, and He shall dispose his way.' I found it in Saint Augustine."

"Steps? Like moves?"

"A kind of game." He laughed. "Funny. That's when I started the beard. I can't get used to him dead, though. It was like he had his life in layaway and couldn't meet the payments."

"Dewey," she said, unbelieving. "Dewey Rabinowitz."

"Wonderful," he agreed. "In Hebrew it would be Dovid. My mother is an Anglophile."

"And what's Jeffrey for?"

"Judah."

"Really? Are there any others? Jessica? Veronica?"

"No. It seems I tipped her uterus coming down."

She woke on the rollaway cot in Sue Ellen's room, heavy with her favorite nightmare. A corner of the shade was flapping monotonously; she had incorporated the sound into the telephone dial of her dream. All night she had sought her mother by plane and train and Hudson Tube. Doors would not open, machinery went berserk and in the final agonizing frame she fought to call her on the phone, but her fingers were child fingers, stubby and soft, and she hung there by her fingers while the stubborn machinery grated, ticking. All her strength could not pull the numbers around.

It was too early to get up. Sue Ellen made soft blubbery noises in her sleep. They were incipient snores. Robin guessed she did not dream at all of the Welfare mothers she carried on her department clipboard. Sue Ellen was a sensible girl, she sorted out in the daytime and was cheerful and compliant in the evening and all night slept the sleep of the just.

She tried to put herself back to sleep with recipes, reviewing several and assembling the ingredients. In her eighth year there was taffy, which had to be boiled to the light-crack stage and pulled between buttered fingers until the whiskery mass yielded and grew opaque in color and became a crystal ribbon. There was a Scandinavian noodle pudding for which she marshaled currants and eggs, sugar, butter and cheese and sour cream and grated lemon rind which she beat together in a large yellow bowl while the noodles boiled. Mostly she was in Toivo's kitchen doing this. She dozed off while putting it in the oven and woke an hour later, refreshed, having done her mothering.

Jeff had put the coffee on in the still-redolent kitchen. While it perked they sat opposite each other at the porcelain table and she sneezed three times. No one else was up.

"Have you got any yeast?" she asked.

He rummaged in the refrigerator, a woolly man in a brown bathrobe that was raveling at the sleeves. The sensation she had was poignant and inexact: it was the humble frayed cloth; it was the memory of a brown-varnished kitchen. He emerged flapping two crumpled foil packs. She sniffed them. They were stained with pickle juice but otherwise intact.

While Jeff cleared away the debris of last night's glasses, she undertook her act of love.

First the sponge of yeast in water barely warm enough to say its absence on the inside of her wrist. Then the scalded milk, butter swimming in it. Beating in the flour till the dough climbed the blades of the electric beater and when she slowed the revolutions, the batter flew off softer than cow flops into the tilted bowl. And working in more flour, a mist of talcum, till the whole sticky mass came together to be turned out for kneading.

Jeff sucked his pipe as she punched, slapped, and folded.

"I love what they call it," she said. "It sounds so Anglo-Saxon. You know, medieval."

"Kneading? It has a Germanic root. The same as knob and knoll and gnocchi, I think. And probably knackwurst."

"All a bunch of bumps," she grunted. And finishing, set the dough to rise on top of the radiator. "That's it," she said, holding up her floury hands. "You'll get three loaves from that."

"What do you call it?" He was unsticking her fingers, picking the webs of dough from between them.

"Sesame egg twist."

And now he was holding both her hands in his. "Sesame egg twist," he repeated. "Robinowitz." She was gathered in against the brown bathrobe and his beard was rustling against her face. "You've just made the Friday night bread, Robinowitz. You've just made challah."

5

Opening the Door
on Sixty-second Street

THE YEAR Jeffrey Rabinowitz was sixteen, his grandfather died at the Seder table. That is, he slumped over the ceremonial plate with its horseradish root and lamb bone and roasted egg, a sprig of parsley in his hand, and had to be helped into the living room to lie down on the horsehair sofa. An elderly doctor, summoned from his own Passover festivities in an apartment upstairs, had laid his ear to the old man's naked chest and pronounced the flutter of his heart to be only a little arrhythmia brought on by excitement.

Nevertheless, Jeff's grandfather died on West End Avenue before the eight days of matzoh were over.

"Did you finish the service? I mean, after he slumped over like that?" Robin wanted to know.

"I think we must have," Jeff said. "Because every year since, I catch myself thinking, we opened the door for Elijah and the Angel of Death entered in. You know, it's the Angel of Death who's supposed to pass over the houses. Instead, he came for Grampa."

It was important to be on time; he was hustling her from the airport terminal, where he had gone to fetch her, to a cab.

"It was always such a joke, opening the door for Elijah. Dewey used to pull rank on me. Being the younger son meant I had to ask the four questions and he got to yank the door open with a flourish. Dewey always said we wouldn't know him if he came, Elijah. He'd never get past the doorman, he used to say."

"Well, he was right, I guess. Now everybody says it about Jesus. When I was little I used to wonder how Jesus could put a coat on."

"Why not?"

"Over his wings, I mean."

"I thought you meant he couldn't fold his arms back down."

"Well, that too. But Unitarians don't talk much about the crucifixion. Our Jesus didn't transfigure."

"Dewey had three apparitions of Elijah in his lifetime. Chariot and all."

"Was God driving?"

"I don't know. When he described it, though, I could see it too. It was a fiery buckboard, all right. Something like Pegasus pulling a hansom cab in Central Park."

The driver cheated a crosstown light and edged between two trucks. They were quiet a minute, considering.

"It must be awfully hard now," Robin said finally. "For your parents, I mean, having the holiday without Dewey."

"In a way, it's easier than his visions and things. They always hated surprises."

His parents were old, he told her. His mother was forty-five when he was born.

"But that's incredible! You're lucky you're not a mongoloid."

"Well, I missed it by a percentage point. My mother was married before. But they never had any children. I think we came as a great shock to her. And my father was one of those

lingering bachelors who finally gave in. He can be very charming, but you always feel he was dragooned into the system. It's
hard for him to cope with family life."

Before dinner there was schnapps in the living room—Scotch
in the palest violet glasses. Only the men partook. Robin in-
ferred that women did not take their whiskey neat and shook
her head when the tray went round.

Jeff's mother had blue hair and blue harlequin glasses. Her
face was childish and well kept with sweet small features, the
skin finely wrinkled. Robin thought of a silk nightgown that
wanted ironing. She wore four rings.

"It just lifts my spirits to have you young people around," she
said, settling her plumpness with a little bounce. "I think a Seder
is more *fun* when you can set a full table. Jeffrey and Dewey
always brought their Christian friends home, we encouraged
that, didn't we, Harris?"

"My wife prides herself on her Christian friends," Harris
Rabinowitz pronounced equably. He too wore glasses and threw
his head back so that the light glinted off them. What wonderful
hair! Robin thought. All silvery and benign, that's where Jeff
gets it.

"What Daddy means is that the holidays are hard when
there's been a death," Mrs. Rabinowitz went on. "You know
about Dewey, of course. He was the *best* baby. He went potty
before he was a year old. Jeffrey here was impossible to train.
You just never could catch him. He'd go in a corner behind the
piano and grunt—I swear it was just to defy me. We used to say
we'd have to send him off to college with Dydee Service."

"Now Clara, does Macy's tell Gimbel's?" Harris Rabinowitz
rumbled.

"Mother has a compulsion to tell all," Jeff said. His voice was even. Robin couldn't tell whether he despised or enjoyed her candor.

"Never mind, never mind," she said. "I'm sure Miss Parks wants to see us as we are."

Miss Parks shoots sparks, Robin thought fiercely, but touched thumbs in her lap.

"I suppose you're wondering where the hors d'oeuvres are," Jeff's mother said. "Usually we have hot and cold ones. But tonight there's so much ceremonial food. Jews don't know how to drink for pleasure, really. These little shot glasses belonged to my father, they're Bohemian glass, you know. It comes from being uprooted, this attachment to *things.*"

And before they went to the table Robin had heard the history of three paintings, a Bisque figurine, and a pair of silver candelabra. It was the kind of promotional revelation that Robin's grandmother, who was, after all, of the same generation, would have shunned. "Good taste speaks for itself, Binnie," Gran would say. "Only an upstart waves a price tag."

"Ready, everyone?" Clara Rabinowitz trilled. "I'm lighting the candles! Sheila dear, will you say the blessing?"

Sheila Sheprow, Jeff's hugely pregnant cousin, stood at the head of the table like the figurehead of a Norse sailing ship and extended her hands, fingers paired, over the candle flames. "Any day now," Art Sheprow beamed. Her pleasantly freckled face shone as if buttered. Her parents, the Poppers, lined up opposite Robin. Downstream at attention stood the other aunt and uncle, the Szalds. Peter Kramer, who grew pot in the aluminum-foil-lined closet of the apartment on West End Avenue he shared with Jeff, took a white silk yarmulka out of his back pocket, kissed it, and put it on. Robin, who had not bowed her head with the others, caught Mrs. Rabinowitz's frown at this gesture.

"That's very sweet of you, Peter," she said just as Sheila cleared her throat, "but we're very informal here. You don't need a yarmulka on East Sixty-second Street."

The pot farmer took off his skullcap, folded and kissed it, and stuffed it back in his pocket. Art coughed tentatively. And Sheila sang the Hebrew blessing in the clear, unself-conscious tones of a small child.

There was a general edging and tugging of chairs; the assemblage was seated. "Now dear," Clara Rabinowitz instructed Robin, "that was to symbolize the *joy* we feel when we can celebrate this festival in our own homes. Next, Daddy will bless the first glass of wine. It's called the kiddush. Oh Harris, wait! Not everyone is served yet."

Harris semaphored with his eyeglasses up and down the table. After he had spoken his portion everyone lifted his goblet. Robin sipped. Thick and sweet, the wine tasted like fermented grape juice.

"You have to drink all of it, you know," Jeff whispered.

"How many of these are there?"

"Four in all."

But his mother had overheard. Again the wide smile which ended in a little downturning of earnestness. "The four cups symbolize the four promises of redemption, Miss Parks. I forget what each one is, exactly. But on this night even the poorest of the poor were to be provided with enough wine to take part in the ceremony."

"It sounds like Thoreau," Robin said. "You know, the thing about 'none is so poor that he need sit on a pumpkin.' "

But no one knew except Jeff.

They had just gotten into the *Dayenus* when the phone rang.

"*Dayenu*—how would you translate that, Harris?" Clara

asked, while deliberate footsteps could be heard moving offstage to lift the receiver.

"Does Macy's tell Gimbel's?" he grumbled.

" 'It would have been enough,' Auntie," Sheila Sheprow supplied. " 'Sufficient unto the day thereof,' something like that."

It was the other Popper children—Sheila's two married sisters and their husbands—conjoined in San Francisco to wish the family Good Yontev. Everyone in turn, except for Peter Kramer and Robin, queued up at the living-room extension. The senior Poppers hurried upstairs to monitor the flow of conversation from the bedroom.

Left to themselves, Robin peeked ahead in the Haggadah. Sixty pages to go, but a lot of it was music.

Peter furtively lifted a napkin, slid out a wheel of matzoh, and stood in a corner by the china cabinet munching. "Starved," he explained. "Anyway, we're very informal here."

"That bothered you."

He shrugged. "She has her meaningful rituals, I have mine."

"Why did you kiss it?"

"You have your crucifix and I have my grandpa's yarmulka."

"But Peter! I'm a Unitarian."

"So? A Unitarian's nothing but a homesick Christian."

"There will be a short wait for all seats," Jeff said coming back. "Sheila is reviewing her pregnancy long distance. She's up to the seventh month now. How's it going, Robinowitz?"

"Miss Parks to you."

"That's just Mother's way of indicating that you haven't been divinely elected," Jeff said. "Don't let it get you." But he looked unhappy; diminished somehow inside the frame of his curly hair and beard.

She relented. "No, it's very interesting, really. I *like* it. And

I like having your mother explain things."

Between bouts of exegesis the service proceeded communally with each member reading a part. The Szalds shared one pair of bifocals, which they passed back and forth between them like a dish of olives. Kramer, discountenanced by the English, chose each time to deliver his portion in Hebrew. Mrs. Rabinowitz promptly translated by way of reproof.

Symbols exalted her. She explained the parsley—gratitude to God for the fruits of the earth—the horseradish root, a warty phallus that made Robin think of John Donne's mandrake poem —the bitter lot of the Jews in Egypt—the charoses, unexpectedly delicious—mortar for the bricks the Jews made when they were the Pharoah's slaves. And did Miss Parks know why the matzoh was scored in perforations? (Does Macy's tell Gimbel's?) To keep the dough from rising and swelling.

During the dinner itself, conversation found its urban level. The Szalds reported a mugging; they alternated details like a responsive reading. The Poppers brought up landlords. Art Sheprow defended rent strikes, busing, and peaceful acts of civil disobedience to disrupt the war machine.

"Have you ever done it?" Robin asked him. "Sat in, I mean?"

"I'd like to. But I can't risk arrest with Sheila in this condition."

Harris Rabinowitz sighed obtrusively. Conviviality sat heavily on him. "The schwartzehs, the schwartzehs," he said. "Between the schwartzehs and the dog-do the whole city is a slum. When I was a young man we went up to Harlem to hear jazz. Portaricka was a foreign country. A nice Jewish girl if she had to work went into teaching. Now she goes to CCNY and gets raped in the ladies' room."

Robin, prepared to despise him, was startled when he turned

to her in supplication. "Don't get me wrong, young lady. You think I'm just a kvetch, a complaining old man. You think I'm some kind of a right-wing fanatic. But I want to tell you, I loved this city before it turned into a jungle. I was born here, I grew up in the Bronx in what they call a semidetached. I had all kinds of neighbors, Italians, Polish people, even some coloreds. I went with all kinds, we had respect. The trouble with today is, there's no respect."

After dessert, they returned to the Haggadah. Art Sheprow, slightly flushed, read the grace and the company supplied the responses. When he came to "The door is opened for Elijah," there was a pause. Mrs. Rabinowitz unfolded a handkerchief and dabbed her eyes.

"We don't have to do this part," Jeff warned.

"No, Jeffrey, I *want* to. I want *you* to do it." To Robin, she said, "It makes us all remember Dewey. Dewey *saw* Elijah, you know. Oh, no one ever believed him, I didn't at the time, but maybe he knew something we didn't. Dewey was such a bright child! Up until the eighth grade he always got all A's on his report card. Of course every night he read the same fairy tales over and over in his bed, we should have guessed that he was troubled, boys don't generally read fairy tales, but he loved them so! He identified. He was the frog who was going to turn into a prince. When all along he was the prince already."

Robin felt as if she were being forced to witness an act of indecent exposure.

Jeff stumbled from the table like a man fighting his way out of a hidden swamp. The front door was opened; the normal raw sounds of traffic swept in.

"O Praise the Lord all ye nations," Art Sheprow recited dubiously. After "Hallelujah!" there was the sucking sound of the door refilling its space. The latch clicked and Jeff returned to his seat with a marvelous show of self-possession.

This is what Robin read on his face: I shat in my pants to the age of four on purpose behind the piano. I played stoopball and kept porno magazines under the mattress and got C's in Latin. I have opened the door on Sixty-second Street and closed it again on the usual arrangement of furniture. It is not part of the divine plan that Elijah appear to Jeffrey Rabinowitz.

They went on into the Psalms. "Out of distress I called upon the Lord. He answered me with great enlargement," Sheila recited. "Oh, my God!" she said, pushing her chair back. Now she was standing, saying, "Oh, my God, my God, I'm wetting my pants!"

In that suspended moment Mrs. Szald took off the bifocals and handed them to Mr. Szald, who put them into his breast pocket. In her haste to get out of her chair Mrs. Popper knocked over a wine glass and Art Sheprow unaccountably buried his face in his hands.

It was all happening in slow motion like a baseball replay; an awkward out-of-sequence pushing back of chairs against the heavy pile of the carpet, stick figures captured in various stages of arising, and a pool of wet unmistakably darkening the Aubusson.

Clara Rabinowitz found the first words. "It's all right, Sheila dear, your water just broke. Your water just broke and you're going to have your baby tonight."

"Let me take your shoes," Robin offered. Sheila stepped out of her navy pumps. Little puddles spilled from them.

Mrs. Popper, seeking equilibrium, exclaimed, "Isn't it lucky you're going to Doctors Hospital? You're already on the East Side, darling. Isn't that the luckiest thing?"

"Oh, get me a towel, somebody!" Sheila wailed.

"Come on, old man. You're not going to be sick or something," Jeff said, steering the father-to-be from the table.

Mr. Popper called a cab. Coats were located and handed around. Sheila tucked a hand towel into her panties.

And the door on Sixty-second Street opened for the second time.

❋6❋

The Consciousness-Raising of Robin Parks

AFTER THE END of the affair with Toivo, Robin left behind a silly white fake-fur robe he had once bought her to flap in the closet like some long-sleeved ghost. She wanted the pale-eyed economist to pass it every morning on his treasure hunt for a flannel shirt or a clean pair of khakis. To see the hem floating above him as he burrowed behind the hiking boots to retrieve a sneaker. Dust balls would have gathered among the shoes and the hanging white ghost have gone lamb yellow by now. But it wasn't the small act of vengeance against Toivo, it wasn't Jeff's tweedledum aunts and uncles, or the pasteboard holy world of his mother that made her decide to have her consciousness raised. She went in search of conviction the way Lancelot set out to find the Grail. What she wanted was some formal symmetry to go by. A pattern as orderly as Latin, an important place to put her fealties. For the time being she put them into the quest.

There were twelve women registered in her consciousness-raising group, but usually only seven or eight of them appeared around the teakwood table on Monday and Thursday evenings. Beryl, a clinical psychologist, owned the house off Brattle Street in which they met. She was a stylish woman in her forties with sky-blue eyelids and frosted hair and she insisted from the outset that she was not the group leader.

"I'm only here to pour the coffee," she told them.

Nevertheless, they all looked up to her.

Practically everyone else in the group had had previous psychotherapy.

"The Freudian movement is at the mercy of its practitioners," a lady lawyer from Ropes and Gray said. "Every shrink I had resented me, I was a castration threat to them. God! I'm sick and tired of being treated like an amateur male."

"Well, this is self-therapy," Beryl explained, passing the cups. "We're here with one unifying purpose, to increase our self-awareness. Other groups are politically oriented, or socio-something or other. Ours is personal. We're here for an overhaul. We're committed to change."

There was a nurse who was afraid to nurse. "Every time I have to give a shot my hands shake like a wino's."

A buyer for a department store chain sympathized. "I know what you're going through. I'm so terrified of planes that I take along a hammer and an axe to break the window in case we ditch over water. It's terrible because I have to fly a lot. I just live on Librium. And besides, the tools are heavy."

Robin thought it was better to be afraid and keep on going than not to go at all.

"You have to put a certain face on things," someone else offered. "If you give in once, it's harder the next time."

But there were other ways of failing. "It's the repetition that grinds you down, there's no way to get rid of all the mindless drudgery. The tables keep on getting dusty the way spinach gathers sand. And no machine is going to wipe a baby's bottom."

"But there's a certain amount of drear in everyone's life," Robin protested. "Look at a bank teller counting out fives and tens in his cage all day. Or a subway motorman. And executives, with a bottle in the desk, they're bored too."

"I'm not talking about boredom," the young mother insisted. "I can stand to be bored, it's part of the Puritan work ethic. It's the exploitation, the system I'm getting at. Even the motorman has some mastery."

"Aren't we all talking about fulfillment?" a middle-aged woman who had been an actress wanted to know. "I played Rosalie in *The Children's Hour,* you remember, Rosalie is the innocent one that Mary blackmails into lying."

At least Beryl knew.

"I was nineteen, on the subway circuit, I played as far away as Atlantic City. The girl who played Mary was the daughter of a New York publisher, she took me home once for the weekend. They lived on Park Avenue in this fantastic duplex, the wallpaper had gold fleur-de-lis on it. And the maid unpacked for me, me with one tacky little suitcase, she laid out my one poor little dress. It was banker's gray with a white collar and little buttons. And I hated that dress, I wanted to cut it up with fingernail scissors. At dinner Mrs. Fielding asked me what my father did. I told her he was on the WPA. Of course it was my sense of the dramatic that made me do that. Actually, he worked in the post office. But you know? Even though I was terrified, I was alive. Nothing in my life since came up to that time."

At the third session Beryl said to Robin that she had to get over her habit of standing outside things like a child at the zoo. "There you are," Beryl said not unkindly, "watching to see how the camels do it with their humps and all. The important thing is how *you* do it and how it makes you feel. You can't be a voyeur all your life."

The trouble was, Robin *felt* like a child at the zoo. In everybody else's anguish, she was certain, lay the key to her own. She was trying to expand, like a gas balloon.

They talked about their mothers, who had taught them a life style that was inappropriate for them to fill. They talked about being taught to lose because that was how women win, by losing. The sessions were full of references to vicarious gratification and low status and depression and the Virgin Mary syndrome.

"My mother is an alcoholic," Robin said when pressed. "I hardly ever lived with her after I was four or five. My grandmother and my great-aunt brought me up."

"But that explains a lot!" Beryl said enthusiastically.

"It doesn't matter, of course you *love* them," the Ropes and Gray lawyer said. It was plain that she doubted it. "We all love our mothers or their surrogates. Deep feelings, love, hate, rejection . . ." She trailed off, uncertain.

Cornered, Robin attempted to explain about Gran. "For instance, the way she goes on making lists. She thinks there are still girls who want to come out, for God's sake, she still says things like tuxedos and tails. If debutantes have to get stuck with a ceremony they want rock and soul music, or a documentary film with a group discussion of dynamics afterward. And my grandmother goes back to those really incredible parties on the North Shore with enormous marquees and receiving lines and two orchestras and lots of champagne. She wants to run things like a Monopoly game. There she is, still stuck on Park Place, thinking she owns all of Boardwalk."

"Why do you let her manipulate you? That's a very unhealthy

situation, a young girl shuttling back and forth between two old women. Living in the past that way."

"But I'm the keeper of their stories, don't you see? The custodian of their pasts, I hold them into this century."

"But what was it like?" Beryl persisted. "You intellectualize everything, what was it really like?"

And so Robin remembered dancing class. "It was all Wasp and terribly proper, with white gloves. Even the boys had to wear gloves, at least for the promenade."

"You mean you had to learn how to walk?"

"You were supposed to learn how to come in on the arm of a boy. Any old boy, someone who was assigned to you at the door. My grandmother used to take me there in a taxi, she'd comb out my hair on the way and tell me to keep my shoulders back and make me practice smiling . . ."

There was a general murmur of sympathy.

"And then she'd boot me out of the cab and I'd have to go up the walk alone, knowing she was watching me to see if I stood up straight. What she didn't know was that I had this hysterical astigmatism or something, everything fuzzed over, I couldn't focus."

"But you don't wear glasses," Beryl said.

"No, this was only then. I'd walk in, it was like having a paper bag over my head, the faces all blurred and ran together and of course I was so shy nobody ever wanted to dance with me. I mean, other girls had boy friends. I never had anything but assigned partners."

"Oh God," said the lawyer. "A sex object at twelve."

"No, wait, it was worse. After the promenade I'd go hide in the ladies' room as long as possible. Mrs. Ingalls knew where to look for me. And when it was time to go home, everyone had to get back into this sedate circle with the same boy they'd started out with. And Mrs. Ingalls, that horrible old Mrs. Ingalls would take me by the hand and go around and around the room saying, 'Is this the boy you came with, Binnie? Is this the one, Binnie dear, or this one?' And of course every single one of those nasty simpering little asses would deny he was the one."

"Well, why didn't you tell her?"

"I couldn't see," Robin said simply. "My eyes wouldn't focus and I just couldn't see. I guess I didn't want to."

"Denial," Beryl pronounced. "The defense of denial."

"Finally, my great-aunt got me out of it."

"What did she do? Did she speak to your grandmother?"

"She said," Robin said, remembering exactly, " 'Now Lyddie, since you are so intent on performing a crucifixion, you might as well use a hammer and nails.' "

❋ "THE WHOLE THING sounds like a communal confessional to me," Jeff said when she told him about the group. "If you raise your consciousness any higher, Robinowitz, I'll need a sky hook to hold you down."

"The trouble is," she told him, "I'm a very old-fashioned people. I fiddle away at old-fashioned problems."

"The trouble is, you are a very stiff-necked people. Very Old Testament in fact. What old-fashioned problems?"

She hedged. "Well, something Norman O. Brown says about what it is to be a Protestant. Always looking 'for the one true and literal meaning.' "

"And do you think you'll find it with the Ladies of the Garter?"

"That just shows what kind of a snob you are," she said. "You suffer from male superior objective rationality."

"I don't suffer, I enjoy it."

In the group they were drawing up a Declaration of Sexual

Rights. These included the right to a separate checking account, a list defining separate responsibilities around the house, and the total abrogation of the responsibility to Do It unless they damn well felt like it.

"For God's sake," he said. "It's like making a budget, putting this much in this envelope for the rent and that much for recreation. You make the whole thing sound like a cost-accounting process."

"Well, what if it does? There has to be some way to break down the traditional roles."

"Sometimes tradition is a way of keeping going."

"That's what I mean. Keeping going the traditional, sex-stereotyped way. When partners draw up a marriage contract, they can define their obligations. Nobody gets stuck, they can share the dirty work."

"What about caring?" he asked. "What about doing something for somebody because maybe you love him and never mind whose turn it is?"

"Fine," she said. "That way it's always the woman's turn."

"Robinowitz. How can you keep a score card?"

"Everybody is keeping score all the time anyway. They just don't admit it."

"Is that how it is? Nothing but a fucking baseball game?"

"Call it a baseball game if you want," she said. "If it helps you to put it down that way."

Which was all academic since they were neither living nor sleeping together. She was more or less willing to; in his arms she was ready to be convinced, but he wasn't.

"First you have to get straight in your own mind," he said. "I'm not going to crowd you."

"Anyway, I think I'm frigid." She had not told it to the ladies.

She was intellectually dishonest, a freeloader in the group.

"That's throwing down the gauntlet, Robinowitz," he said. "That's tossing me the challenge all right. You want me to prove to you that you're not, don't you? Well, forget it. That's not the name of the game."

❇ IT WAS LILAC TIME. The consciousness-raisers were discussing liberated orgasms. On Marlborough and Commonwealth the magnolias were sending up their enormous waxy blooms. Robin distrusted both events; they were too showy. She remembered those times with Seavey Stevens in his rooms in Lowell House while his roommate considerately went to a Bogart revival or sat drinking beer in the Oxford Grille, all the while looking at his wrist watch. At least that was what she thought of, the minute hand going round, while she was getting laid. It took her mind off Seavey's physiology texts scattered on the floor where he had swept them in order to make way for their ritual. It took her mind off Tante, approached at fifteen by her new stepfather in a tacky flat in Paris. Tante, whose mother gambled and lost all day under a parasol at the Hippodrome in the Bois.

Sometimes with Toivo, Robin thought she was rowing desperately for an island. She could see the shallows beginning under the boat, could see where the yellow beach sand waited and a thin line of surf was softly falling and then the current carried her offshore again and the orgasm drifted out of reach. In bed there would have been layers and layers to Gran, muslin, linen, silk, for she was a seamless woman of fixed address. No matter that she had married and brought forth Robin's mother; it was deceitful and cowardly for Robin to imprison her on her back. At that moment when lovers turn a little aside fishing a stray hair out of their mouths Robin was always putting the wrong things together. For instance, just this side of coming, her long-dead father's bow ties jutted rakish and crooked in her head.

The thing was, and she took herself to task for it, she was deficient in the kind of generous passion that causes girls of sixteen to rush headlong into the act and come away from it exalted. She had gone to bed with Seavey in the first place to get rid of the nuisance—no, the downright burden—of her virginity. Probably if she had rolled in earlier with one of those Browne and Nichols boys who had tried to seduce her for their honor's sake, any one of those now faceless preppies who had brought to her their chivalrous sexual zeal, she would by now be ready for a more mature vision. A solidly satisfying era of fucking awaited her somewhere in the shallows, she clung to that. Having had a head drummed full of her privileges and good fortunes, she tended always to make excuses for others. *They* could not help it; their shortcomings and nastinesses were the fault of some flaw in their genes or their environment. *She*, on the contrary, could, would, must. She suffered an excessive tact, a fear of causing pain, was brought up to endure rather than offend. Suffer fools gladly, eat what is served you even if it causes you to break out in giant hives later. Shiver rather than demand an extra blanket, allow the hairdresser to cut away inches of your hair rather than wound him with the information that you had requested only a trim. For this her thighs opened. She would, could, must.

"I am too old to have friends who drive," Gran had said, so of course Robin drove her. They had gone alone in an Avis car to Sudbury and Maynard and Lexington to see the lilacs spilling over fences, the azaleas mannerly in doorways. They had come back by way of the Arnold Arboretum for the dogwood and a few proud cherry trees—"Both Washington and Philadelphia put us to shame in this department," Gran affirmed—just as the sun was going down. At the next intersection a thin black man in a blue workshirt jumped into the back seat of the car.

That he was black, that the shirt was a much-laundered blue were the only details Robin could remember afterward. And a dull gleam from the wide-mouthed pistol he waved between them, pressing it over the front seat. She drove where he directed, through city traffic, past tenements and warehouses as the dark sky settled and street lights came on. "Do exactly as he says, Binnie," Gran kept repeating after every instruction and he replied with the softest of slurs, "That's right, lady."

It was important not to think, it was important only to steer, accelerate, brake. Keep two hands on the wheel, listen, obey. Gran sitting straight as an intelligent dog one might take for a ride, breathing in shallow animal gasps. "Down here," he directed. "Watch for that li'l street on the right, see it? Turn off your lights and go down it easy." Robin could see a break between buildings, an alley running behind high, blank-faced factories. She knew he would kill them both in that cul-de-sac. She coasted as if to turn; there were cars up ahead, and magically, people spilled out of a building. "Duck!" she screamed to Gran, and rammed full speed into a row of parked cars. He fired. The bullet pierced the roof at the moment of impact but the explosion was lost in the larger sounds of glassbreak and metal on metal. When she looked up, he had gone, running on sneak-ered feet. She had made a choice, taken a terrible and deliberate risk, could have gotten them both killed. On the other hand, they were marked to die. She knew it. Pleading to be spared in that wet alleyway. It was marvelous how you could lie back at the last minute and depend on instinct. Instinct rode her foot down on the accelerator. The kidnapper was never caught.

The gun came and went in her dreams for weeks but they were soluble nightmares. She was pursued, shot at, she carried her grandmother on her back across a prairie, the same faceless thin man unzipped and would have shot her with his tool but she kicked over a garbage can and he tripped, went sprawling. That he was black in fact and black in her dreams she preferred to pass over. Her unconscious was a faithful reporter; her unconscious was a vile extension of her primitive and repressed prejudice.

Gran took to her bed for three days. She had bruised her elbow on the dashboard when they hit and somehow had bitten her lip so that it bled, but nothing loomed so large as her anger. The truth was, Lydia Latham had wet her pants in terror. "All this could have been prevented, Binnie, if you had only locked the doors," she told Robin. "You were foolhardy to the point of insanity, Binnie, to do such a thing. We could have been killed, both of us. Shot through the head by accident or design when you made us crash." No use to point out that they could have been shot through the head either way. Or raped first and then shot. No use to point out that all this could have been prevented if they had rented the cheaper, two-door model. "Getting our names in the papers like common criminals. And you smiling for the reporters."

Tante had been invited on the outing but suffered just then from a touch of *la grippe*. She stumped over the next day with her cane. "And here's my Binnie," she said hugging Robin. "A true heroine. You kept your head, my girl. Anyone else might have fainted or screamed, but you outwitted him."

Gran turned her head to the bedroom wall and refused to discuss it further. "Subway flowers," she said when Tante had gone. "My life was hanging in the balance and all Tessa can think to do is bring me those nasty wilted tulips from the subway kiosk. I suppose she'll come to my funeral with drugstore candy."

"I wouldn't mind so much if I knew *why,*" Robin said to Jeff that weekend. "I mean, what right does she have to be so angry?"

"Why do you think?"

"First of all, it's the relief," she said. "She expected to be raped and dismembered and she wasn't. She isn't exactly the type to weep for joy."

"Maybe having it all acted out took something away from her," Jeff suggested. "Instead of confirming her worst fears. You say she's always been hysterical on the subject, there was always a rapist on every corner in her fantasy. Well, in a way you wrecked her main chance, awful as it was."

"Damn it," Robin said. "What about me?"

"What *about* you, Robinowitz? You're the conqueror, that's what. You caught the fastest cock in the west and you shot it down."

But she hadn't shot anything and the gunman was still, as the *Globe* said, at large. If he read the papers he knew where to find her. She could not afford to feel for him the compassion that was his due. A clergyman robbed in the pulpit would have said at the parting, shouting to his disappearing back, "Remember, my boy, God loves you." And her gunman would have replied, "God is dead." In the raising of consciousness she had come that far.

Beryl called to express the shocked condolences and congratulations of the group. "We miss you," she said. "When will you be back?"

"Not for a while. I'm going away for the summer."

"Oh, really? With the grandmothers?" Beryl's tone was frosty. It suggested hotel verandas overlooking the ocean. Rainy afternoons in antique shops.

"No. With Jeffrey Rabinowitz. We're going to build a house in the country." She realized she was making up her mind as she went along.

Gran was keenly disappointed. "I had thought we might go to Dune's Head Inn for a few weeks, Binnie. I had even thought we might invite your great-aunt to join us. Her apartment is intolerable in the summer. Needless to say, it would be more than I could bear to take on the burden of her presence all by myself. And this school chum of yours, what did you say her name was?"

"Betty Muhner."

"Muhner, Muhner. New Yorkers, I presume." It was her euphemism for Jew.

"They're Swiss, Gran," Robin lied patiently, having invented a daughter for Jeff's bachelor farmer neighbor.

"Refugees."

"The Swiss were neutral, remember? In both wars."

Of course Tante took the other tack. It was incumbent upon her.

"A month in the country, that's like a stage play, Binnie. Canoes on the water and blackberries as big as your thumb. To wake to the roosters crowing and help with the haying. To live by the laws of nature. O Pioneers!" Tante loved to open her heart at a safe remove.

❋ THERE WAS NO bus depot in the little New Hampshire town. The Trailways disgorged her in front of the library, a one-room brick structure with a rusty cannon on its lawn. Jeff was waiting with a Volkswagen van. He was stockier and more saturnine than she had remembered him in Manhattan. They drove like two strangers in an air pocket of silence over the state road, then up the packed dirt track that climbed Little Mink Hill. The van bumped past Muhner's white farmhouse, his sheep sheds, pastures, pine lots, and barn, and petered out at the edge of a wood lot. A bright blue tent yawned open on its wood platform and the afternoon sun shone into it. A sleeping bag was airing on a branch, humble as a homemade quilt. Ten yards away, an outhouse of raw pine boards smelled as rosinous as a sawmill.

Jeff led her around the homestead. A lean-to for supplies, a Coleman stove, an ice chest. At the well, a crank and bucket. *Life near the bone,* Robin thought, *where it is the sweetest.* At the same time she felt a great premonitory shiver. How had she come to this place to share the dung heap and air mattress of a stranger? *We know but few men; a great many coats and breeches,* Thoreau had also said. He had gone to the woods to live deliberately, to cut a broad swath and shave close. She had gone to the woods to become her own apostle, to escape from plastics and hypocrisy, affluence and old age. It was not a public mission to declare a utopia, but a private ambition to identify, name, re-invent if necessary, the finical self of Robin Parks. On this drumlin where less than two dozen souls now farmed and logged and raised cattle, two thousand patriots had lived in the time of Thomas Jefferson. The emotion of beginning again exalted her. Not deliberately choosing the difficult as if there were no reasons for the easements of technology. But to take up Henry David's crusty admonishment, to be a Columbus to the new continents inside her.

She had not counted on the black flies. No spray or citronella deterred them. They worried pounds off the livestock and walked on the eyeballs of sheep. They crept beneath cuffs and waistbands, burrowed in ears and hair, invaded the mosquito netting to lurk in the sleeping bag and create a torment of bright and lasting itches.

"Stay covered up," Jeff advised, and slathered her with the evil-smelling dip Muhner used on his cattle. The consistency of melted lard, it stood up in droplets on her skin. The constant swarm thinned somewhat and the ragged whine in her ears dimmed. Nevertheless, she went to the outhouse and cried privately, and stayed to stiffen her resolve by reading a few more pages from Sarah Kemble Knight's journal. On October 2, 1704, Sarah had written:

> When we had Ridd about an how'r, wee come into a thick swamp, which by reason of a great fogg, very much startled mee, it being now very Dark. But nothing dismay'd John: Hee had encountered a thousand and a thousand such Swamps, having a Universall Knowledge in the Woods; and readily Answered all my inquiries which were not a few.

It took them a week, using a pinch bar and block and tackle, to move the fallen stones out of the cellar hole. Clearing the trees that had sprung up therein was easier. Jeff left a tall stump of one—a golden birch—to serve as a table. Robin dug daily in the humus to rescue the old bricks for a fireplace and came on a squat blue bottle, all bubbly and seamless. "For ink," Jeff explained. "See? It's hand-blown, probably very old." Later, she was touched to discover it washed clean and filled with Canada may flowers on their tree table. She thought again of Thoreau's aphorism. Coats and breeches did not pick wild flowers.

In ten days she had new muscles and a thrifty attitude toward water. At night Jeff rubbed her aching calves and picked pine needles out of her hair and they read side by side like self-improving Victorians. The Coleman lantern hissed hanging from the ridgepole, making the small comforting sound of water coming to a boil. The summer's first dusty millers stickered themselves to the tent flap. The woods beyond their circle of light gave forth a constant chitter noise, a life that took up its industry after sunset. Under the air mattress in even rows arranged according to thickness Jeff kept his evening library. From it Robin had earlier carried off Madam Knight's diary to the privy. The town history was lodged under her left ear, and next to it a collection of literature of the colonies. Jonathan Edwards' sermons, full of wickedness and uplift, put her directly to sleep, but the record of early settlers was significant to the edge of awesomeness. It delighted her to read that Amos Morseby, the first white child on Little Mink Hill, was born at the river camp, half a mile from where she lay propped on one elbow, the lantern making concentric circles on the page. That same week his father shot an Indian thieving from the granary. She bracketed in William Byrd's journal:

All nations of men have the same natural dignity, and we all know that very bright talents may be lodged under a very dark skin. The Indians by no means want understanding, and are in their figure tall and well-proportioned. Even their copper-colored complexion would admit of blanching, if not in the first, at the farthest in the second generation.

I may safely venture to say, the Indian women would have made altogether as honest wives for the first planters, as the damsels they used to purchase from aboard the ships. It is strange, therefore, that any good Christian should have refused a wholesome, straight bed-fellow, when he might have had so fair a portion with her, as the merit of saving her soul.

To be simplified into a wholesome, straight bed-fellow—how durable it sounded!

On the twenty-second, twenty-third, and twenty-fourth days of her tenure, they woke to a steady downpour. Robin squatted in the lean-to, cooking oatmeal. She was soaked to the knees. As the porridge bubbled, she dropped in a handful of raisins mournfully one by one. Her mother had shaken puffed rice out of a quivering box into a child's bowl on such a succession of days. Rain had rattled the window sash. The bourbon bottle abutted the orange-juice pitcher and it was time to go to school.

"At least there aren't any snakes," Jeff said in his best cheerful voice. "In Africa, every hump in the road was suspicious. The vegetation would just shoot up overnight in the rainy season, big thick green tangles, and snakes everywhere as if they'd come down out of the sky. In the morning you'd shake out your boots to be sure."

Robin put her hands over her ears. "Don't tell me about it, okay?"

Jeff, under a tarpaulin, dried off the VW's spark plugs and they drove to Concord to linger in the hardware store, the supermarket, the wide aisles of Sears Roebuck. They had grilled cheese sandwiches in Howard Johnson's, all oleoed and flattened as with an iron, and settled in with popcorn at a Bob Hope rerun in the movie house in the next block.

"Don't you feel sort of marvelously depraved or something?" she said driving back. It was still raining and patches of ground fog obscured the road from time to time. "I mean, there we were all day on sidewalks and under roofs. Jeff?"

"Mildly."

"Let's stop the car and park," she said. "Let's pull off the road and neck for a while."

"So you can be sixteen again at Brimmer and May? Come on, Robinowitz. What for? We have a private mountain and a waterproof tent to neck in." But he leaned across to pat her knee.

In the next instant he hit the brake. She saw two bright phosphorescences, a pale blond shape that dodged, turned, and ran directly into the nose of the van. There was the slight thud of impact and then they had stopped, one wheel in the soft shoulder.

"A dog. Oh, God!" she moaned.

Jeff was out of the van and across the road before she had opened the door.

"It's a fawn. Christ! I broke its back. It's not dead. Don't look, Robinowitz."

"What are you doing?"

He had clambered back in.

"I've got to finish it. Don't look."

But she followed him, tire iron in his hand, back across the road and she saw him bash the delicate head once, twice with the metal. The blood and brain matter made a sharp stain like oil on the macadam. She went down unexpectedly on one knee and vomited.

"Can't," Jeff said. "Can't just leave it." She heard rather than saw him drag the carcass off the highway. Then the sound of him blowing his nose heavily like an old man. The sound of the tire iron being dragged through tall grass.

Finally he was next to her and they held each other, wet and sour in the fine rain and went back, arms laced tight to the van.

Back on their private mountain Jeff brought water to the lean-to and fired up the camp stove. They stripped and washed and rubbed each other dry.

"O Pioneers!" Robin said shakily in the tent. "Funny, it was
so . . . pale. Speckled, like a baby robin. I thought it would be
browner."

"It was a big one," Jeff said. "For a minute I thought it was
a pony. I've never seen such a big one."

"Poor fawn."

"Poor Robinowitz."

They lay quietly together in the bookless evening and dozed
and woke to clear night. Jeff unbuttoned the tent flap. There
were stars and a breeze methodically lifted and let fall the
canvas.

"Hungry?"

She nodded. In truth she was starved.

He was gone a long time. She lay content with the newly
chilly breeze on her skin and the sounds of his activity in the
lean-to. He brought two mugs of cocoa and a plate of thickly
buttered graham crackers.

"Enough?" he asked, watching her eat.

She was embarrassed by her greediness, licking butter from
her fingers. "It's just right."

"That's what Dewey and I used to have Sunday nights when
the parents were out. We used to see how many times we could
butter the same cracker. You know, licking it off until the
cracker melted under your tongue."

"That's how I used to eat an apple. You keeping putting
peanut butter on the bitten part and keep eating it off to see how
long you can make the apple last."

"Dewey used to drink vinegar," he remembered. "He'd go in
the pantry and swig it right out of the bottle."

She grimaced. "Once I ate a whole pound of cashews in bed.
I stole them in Sage's and never got caught. I used to suck them

by the mouthful until they got so runny you hardly had to chew at all."

But the gluttonies of childhood were making her shy. When he kissed her, her mouth opened under his and then she turned her face away.

"Yes, all right," she said. "I want to, but I told you, I'm not very good at it."

"It's not a College Board exam, Robinowitz. The results don't go to Princeton. It's not something you have to get eight hundred on to get into Radcliffe."

She said into the hollow above his collarbone, "They give you two hundred just for printing your name in the right squares."

"You're so wistful. What's in those squares, baby? What do you want that you think you don't have?"

"Feeling."

"I promise you," he said. "I promise you we won't do anything without feeling. Nothing has to happen. There are no rules, nobody's keeping score."

"*I'm* keeping score, goddam it! Don't you see? I want it to be right."

"Then you have to speak up, Robinowitz. You have to say when it goes wrong. It's not like anesthesia."

"What do I say? 'Stop it, Jeff, it isn't working'?"

"That's exactly what you say."

She laughed. "Well, when I do, you won't hear me. You won't be listening."

"Robinowitz. *I will be listening.* I swear to you I'll listen."

"On Elijah's beard will you swear?"

He raised himself up on one elbow and made a mock sign of the cross. "On the beard of Elijah himself."

She put her fingers in his beard and drew his face down to hers.

And never said. Never had cause to say *stop it.*

They saw the sun come up through the other flap. Naked and chilled except where their bodies touched, they lay side by side and watched first the slow salmon streaks, then the whole bowl of the sun slide up over the farthest hill.

"There's something just right for that," Robin said. "I want to read it to you. It's so right it made me cry the first time I came to it."

"Okay."

"Wait, let me see if I can find it. It's the second book from the left."

He handed it to her. "Who wrote it?"

"Bradford, I think. *Of Plimmouth Plantation.* Here it is." And she flopped over onto her belly and angled the text into the light.

And while he rubbed the bare white bottom of Robin Parks she read in the hour of her newly raised consciousness:

"And though it was very dark and rained sore, yet in the end they got under the lee of a small island and remained there all that night in safety. And God gave them a morning of comfort and refreshing (as He usually doth to His children) for the next day was a fair, sunshining day."

* **Part Three** *

7

Falling Down the Well

ALMOST A YEAR had passed since those fair sunshining days. A year in which New Jersey had been slaughtered and hung and divided in commercial portions, a year in which Jeffrey Rabinowitz had not been on the list. Gran was plainly restless in the wake of Tante's failed marriage and the all-but-useless second surgery. She had withstood Beth's visit and held Miss Barnum at bay and most equably seen them off to another san. Now she was determined to salvage something of the summer. What she remembered most vividly was the North Cape cruise of '48 when Brooks Latham in a checkered cap was at her side and they took ten turns each noonday on the upper deck before going in for luncheon at the captain's table.

"Your grandfather liked his nip of akvavit in the lounge," she told Robin. "The purser used to bring it to him on a special tray while I went in to freshen up. He was a handsome man, your grandfather, with a wonderful erect carriage. People turned to admire the way he walked. I don't suppose you can remember him," she trailed off accusingly.

Robin remembered a wide, red face and a silver tooth set back in it. Also a sharp smell she later knew was whiskey. "Of course

I can, Gran," she lied. "He used to make me rabbits out of his handkerchief. As big and white as dinner napkins. And the magic watch, you know, that flew open when you pressed a button." Details that had been handed on. They were smooth with retelling.

Mollified, Gran served the asparagus. "The hollandaise is just this side of curdled," she charged. "I don't know, Binnie. I can't seem to keep adequate kitchen help any more."

Robin tasted. "It's just a little lemony, that's all," she soothed. "And the asparagus is delicious. I always love this time of year when the good fresh vegetables come in season."

"Fortunately at the last minute," Gran was saying. "Cancellations . . . two outside cabins on the top deck. They call them verandas nowadays. It will be good for Tessa, after all her disappointments. We shall have a last nostalgic crossing before these monstrous jets—what are they called? Seven-elevens?"

"Seven-forty-sevens, Gran."

"Yes, well, before they bankrupt the sailing ships entirely. Since you are absolutely determined to abandon us, Binnie," she added, "I have booked only the two cabins. I would of course be more than *delighted* to have you share mine."

Thirty-four days to Copenhagen, the North Cape, and the fiords with a boatful of widows all dressing for dinner. All with lockets and brooches that hung down in their cleavages. "No, I'm going to study," Robin said. "I've decided. Either I'll go on for a Ph.D. in English next fall or I'll take up something else in graduate school."

"But whatever for?"

"For the future." It came out more harshly than she had intended.

"All very admirable, Binnie. But I must warn you that this high seriousness of yours is making you a bit . . . formidable. Unapproachable, almost. After all, there should be something frivolous in your life at your age. Some young man, some evenings under the bright lights." She gestured vaguely in the direction of the chandelier, which looked distinctly cloudy. "I must remind Helen before I go to get at that with the sudsy ammonia."

"Ammonia does wonders with crystal," Robin said, determined to deflect the conversation. "When does your boat sail?"

"A week from today. Far too soon to make a decent preparation, I'm afraid. Not that Tessa will make the smallest effort to put her clothes in order. You may not agree with me, Binnie, but I feel she's failed considerably since her ordeal."

"But she's very brave," Robin offered, taking up the dance. She could agree and demur simultaneously.

"Oh, yes, she's *brave,*" Gran said grimly. "The bravado of stubbornness, I've put up with it for sixty years."

Robin examined the asparagus stems.

"Of course you'll come to New York to see us off?"

Sentence had been passed; it was lighter than usual.

"Of course."

The day before she was to deliver the two old ladies to the *S. S. Scandia,* Robin returned to the college to clean out her office. Jeff had come down to see her. She sat in the old oak swivel chair; he stood at the window with all the dust motes of Boston Harbor flying through the sunlight behind him, like the angels from Bishop Berkeley's pinhead.

It was not the best place to tell him, Robinowitz to Rabinowitz. Still, it was *her* place, the white ring from Tante's avocado plant one scar among many on the battered desk top.

She would not have him for a lawful wedded spouse, she was inadequate, she said, to marriage.

"Inadequate? Everybody feels inadequate."

"That's easy for you to say, Jeff. That's one of those meaningless pseudo-existential remarks men make to women before the entrapment." She fiddled with the stapler, opening and closing its maw. Axel could have been inside it. "You have a career, you're trained to do something."

"Career!" He threw up his hands in a large gesture of despair.

She went on at him. "There are two different realities in marriage; one for men and another for women. Married men live longer. They're more successful, they earn more money than bachelors. But single women are healthier and live longer than married women. Those are sta*tis*tics, Jeff. Now what do you deduce from that?"

"Fuck statistics. I'm talking about you and me, not some shoddy *Ms.* magazine survey."

"Oh, sure! Put it down any way you can. Well, *I* deduce that housework and marriage literally make women sick!"

But he was gathering up his dignity in two fists. "Far be it from me, Robinowitz, to sicken you."

"No, don't you see? It doesn't matter how much I love you, I can't follow you around and be a little English instructor for the rest of my life. At this point I don't even know what I want to be. Maybe I'll go to law school or get a degree in social work. I don't know. I think I'd like to write."

"Marvelous," he said. It was totally uninflected. "Why not?"

She was fiddling with the postage scale now, weighing out paper clips. Twenty-four of them made half an ounce.

"Here's why not. You're asking me to make the supreme

accommodation. Psychologically, marital power belongs to the higher earner, the higher-status job. That's *you*. Even in two-career families it's the woman who ends up accommodating to the man."

"Will you for God's sake stop fiddling with that stuff? You can't weight and measure and clip everything together in a neat package, Robinowitz. We don't fit in a package. You can't put us in a file drawer or on a chart."

"Nevertheless," she said. "How hard do you want to try to get away from sex roles?"

"Me? I don't want to play any role. I just want some continuity in my life. I'd like to tie the end of it back to the beginning. With you."

She said, trying to keep the tears out of her voice, "I think we should consider breaking up. You're too much for me, Jeff. I want to come into my own and I don't even know where it is with you around to lean on."

His cheeks were clown white against the dark of his beard. "You're asking me to get out of your way."

She found she could still nod her head.

At the door he said, "I'll write to you."

"Yes."

"And you'll write back?"

She swiveled around to face him, tears streaking her cheeks. Let him see. "Yes. Of course."

"You don't know," he said, leaving. "You don't know anything about sex roles. I would have taken the baby to work half the time."

❈ A FEW DAYS LATER she received, registered mail, a large manila envelope. There was a letter inside, and a sheaf of lined pages torn from a Harvard Coop copybook.

"Robinowitz," Jeff had written, "I think this is the last thing I can do before I leave you to come into your own (may your kingdom come speedily). I'm going away for three months, but I have plowed and planted the garden up country in case you decide to stay there for a while. I would like to think of you as being there, although I have no rights in this matter. This is the journal I kept for a year or so in the Peace Corps. It may destroy some illusions you have about me, my career and my training. Just possibly it may make you see how the life you lead is not something that gets put on your back early like a hump, as if the best you can do is to try to wear it gracefully. Although it is no inducement, I think you can be anything. I realize that people don't blunder into having babies any more, but I meant what I said about half the time."

She folded the letter into neat thirds, automatically, and went back to grading the last overdue themes of the semester. *Antecedent,* she wrote in the margins. *Spelling. Fragmentary sentence. No such word.* At three o'clock she delivered the themes to the secretary's office, and turned in her keys. She walked to the farthest corner of the campus and there on a park bench, in view of the greasy bay, with the wheel and scream of gulls imitating the jets that landed and took off from the airport opposite, she took out the copybook pages.

✻ "I AM FALLING into the Peace Corps," Jeff had begun his journal on the day after Easter in his twenty-second year, three Easters before he was destined to meet Robin Parks.

I am falling into the Peace Corps the way Mark Twain gets rid of his used-up characters in *Pudd'nhead Wilson* by having them fall into a back-yard well. My application is in order and they're running a check on me. They don't know how indomitably stupid I feel in grad school. I look back on the books I've read and the information I've taken up by capillary action and I wonder where it all went to. What happened to the calm reasoned approach? The common bond, the I-Thou relationship, the lectures by important professors? The hours of critical reading in Widener, the all-day sessions in the Design School studio, those clean well-lighted places that promised order and system and productivity? I've lost my excitement, the edge of sharpness, I make more mistakes drafting or calculating on the slide rule than I used to. Maybe I'm sick, not just in this anemic spiritual sense, but in some deeper way. Let it be. The Peace Corps will be my well.

❋ A WEEK HERE at home and Dewey was up all night again, not mumbling and pacing because he knows then the parents can hear him—the back part of his head is terribly sane, it operates on instinct like an ant cantilevering a dead beetle over an obstacle—just sitting at his desk doing some sort of anxious housekeeping with his papers. He knows I know he hasn't slept now for forty-eight hours, but he came down this morning to breakfast and punctured his fried eggs with one fork tine the same way he used to when he was ten or twelve and spread the yolk with a butter knife that same lovely disgusting way just to put me off from saying what he knows I know. He's breaking up again. You sit across from him and he smiles and doesn't speak and you know he is having those murderous two-way arguments in his head. It must be exhausting, chasing back and forth from one hemisphere to the other that way, taking up the opposite part. I think it must be two equations talking. The left side is always the loser, I can see the blue vein in his temple start to pulse and it looks like Waterman's Ink about to burst. Anyway, there goes Dewey, schizophrenia here we come, that was the last shrink's reasoned diagnosis. I've never understood why they can't see what I see in him, his head running with molasses and all the molasses at the boiling point. The rage runs him downhill until he just falls apart from insomnia. It's Ma's insomnia of course. Hers was always social, an exquisitely controlled punishment she'd visit on us. Now she's worried herself awake right into Dewey's brain.

✻ APRIL IN Cambridge is full of the chaos of Eliot. The dead land, the dull roots bit. I want to behave like a tree, staying in balance because the symmetry is necessary, yet putting the roots down further and further underground as a way of holding on even if blown over. As dull as that, is my ambition. Meanwhile, I'm reading up on Africa, since that seems to be where I'm going. Also, I can use my French a bit there. The other reason is that I'm one of your average ordinary idealists humping around with his white man's burden and if you're going to backpack around with that strapped on, you might as well backpack it in the most underdeveloped place. Which is still Africa, in the boonies. Everyone knows how we—for we, read the Youth of America—long to establish profound important communication between ourselves and others, how we want to express and relate, perceive and accept, pursue common goals for the common weal. How boring it all is! I am a Sears Roebuck catalogue of my generation. No one is surprised to hear any more about the plastic packaged industrial society of the U.S.A. or the bitterness we feel in the face of it. What *is* surprising is that any of us feel a sense of duty toward the world as it is, the Wasps with their *noblesse oblige* and me with my own personal

backpack thing, though it's contaminated with the divine elec-
tion of being a son in Zion. When you say Peace Corps you get
two reactions. Half the population goes all starry-eyed and you
feel like a hypocrite. The other half acts like you'd just passed
a great blue fart; the PC! Rotten to the core. I suppose since
Camelot, the truth lies somewhere in between. I am running
away from Harvard and from Dewey and from a rising (there's
a pun) feeling of impotence with Laura, who sleeps with me like
a wife every Wednesday and Saturday, even while she knows it
will all come to nothing.

❉ I'M NOTICING everything New England this year as if it were
for the first, or the last, time. Climbed Mount Monadnock on
Sunday, where spring is barely started, going up the mountain
six inches a day, and feel an advance nostalgia for it all. I leave
right after my last exam for three months indoctrination in the
Virgin Islands. It's to be language and culture and just the
physical process of getting used to the tropics. If I get through
that, there's a week's furlough and then I'm off to Africa, to the
Ivory Coast to do something they call "rural animation." So
help me. In my head I see a whole bunch of artists hunched over
their drawing boards, making little furry black cats or dogs
move forward by repositioning their legs. That's how racist my
unconscious is. I'm nervous about being a reformer. If I tell the
truth about my feelings to people I come off sounding like a
fanatic. Laura looks at me queerly. Sidelong is the word. She has
a talent for deep and sustained sidelongs. Her irises slide over
like pinballs and I get so defensive that I start reciting Camus
or Dorothy Day or the Declaration of Independence to her. All
my veneer is coming unstuck. Sometimes when I'm with her I
don't know who I really am, which is the problem. It isn't that

she's without aspirations, she has thousands of them but they lack social content, like playing a purer flute or seeing her untitled poems in print in a really major quarterly. So I guess at the me which will stir her up, and then I create it in her eyes. I'm witty or philosophical, I'm intimate or detached, obscene or Puritanical, whatever the audience of herself requires. You can see the end of this thing. She of course thinks the PC is a species of insanity.

I tell her Camus says, "It is possible to fall in love every once in a while. Once is enough, after all. But it is not possible to be a militant in one's spare time." This is designed to make me a hero.

"Militant!" she says. It is invested with the tone of "transvestite"—pity and disgust.

I am patient and supremely detached. I tell her the way Camus says *militant* is the way Dorothy Day says *Bride of Christ* for the True Church. "Though she is a harlot at times, she is our Mother." This is a deliberate ploy, because Laura is a relaxed Catholic.

"Fuck that," she says. "You only love it because it's so innocently Oedipal."

All this is delivered sidelong, this liberated, at-home-in-the-world stuff. I pretend to be very sure of myself. It's a lousy kind of foreplay.

But sometimes when I've finished swimming a half mile or done some terribly orderly calculations of bridge spans and stresses, or even just taken a good crap, I have such a deep sure wordless knowledge of where I end and the world begins, and then I know that compassion has to outweigh doctrine wherever you put yourself.

❉ ST. CROIX is rather like Connecticut, the shape of it, the cows, and fields of grasses that never seem to turn into hay. We are housed in little screened cabins on one corner of a large plantation, looking across at a ruined Danish castle, crumbled down from the days of sugar fortunes and slaves. The blacks go barefoot, they pad around us with an air of awful servility. It's true we are only tourists here, a bunch of well-fed, upper-middle-class, college-educated earnest do-gooders. Nevertheless, we are not to be despised. Actually, it's cheating to write in this journal in English. The first thing we had to do on arrival was to take a vow to speak and think only in French. Everybody is so pathetically eager that there have hardly been any lapses. You get the inflection really fast; for instance, today swimming I stepped on a sea urchin and heard myself saying aiee! instead of ouch. The first French dream I had wasn't very satisfying— there were a bunch of nuns in an airport chattering and I couldn't understand what they were saying, but consoled myself with the knowledge that they were Canadian and I couldn't be expected to unravel their accent. In the next one I picked up a sentence here and there: *"l'autobus va d'une ville à l'autre,"* for example, when I am wandering around an unknown city strongly reminiscent of Fredericksted but with the gold dome of the Boston State House sticking up on the horizon. The quality of the French dream is uneasy and imperfect, full of misunderstood nuances, like the first wet dream. Something warm and sticky is under you, yet a part of you, but you don't quite associate this slumber-answer with jacking off. Dewey said it was the emanation of my Martian twin speaking through me. I was hideously embarrassed by the bottom sheet, not that anyone ever mentioned it. The parents were close to sixty then, but you'd think my mother with her forever-young cult might have applauded my coming of age. I wonder with a daughter if she would have admired the first blood. I could understand the old man's reluctance—does Macy's tell Gimbel's? Even now I remember the shock of first seeing him naked, him casually undressing to go swimming up at Candlewood, and me riveted with attention. All that curly hair and those wooly mammoth balls, I thought they might burst out and fall on the floor. And me with a little shriveled pink pouch. I felt it and it was empty. A naked father is a fearsome thing. I don't think I even dared imagine my mother.

✻ THERE ARE six girls here, all training to go into public-health programs. One of them is named Joe Ella Marvell, a direct descendant of Andrew, no doubt. She's from Rome, Georgia, and she's all fringey like a daffodil. Sheepdog bangs and puffy blouses and the sturdiest legs, none too long, which are unaccountably appealing. Her father is a professor of anesthesiology at Emory and her mother is a social worker for the state. Between the spinal taps and the battered children, Joe Ella is at home with all kinds of gore. Maybe that's why she has a research intellect. She is mildly interested in pursuing a lower infant mortality rate and eradicating sleeping sickness and all of that, but her real subversive goal in the PC is to examine the effect of the tropical climate on the puberty cycle. The physiology of it, not the rest of that rot, she said, meaning clitoridectomies and the facial scarring of males, a lecture we had just come from. Both still stubbornly practiced, by the way, and countenanced by their enlightened governments.

✻ A LETTER from Dewey about acoustical waves. I can only quote: "It has now been shown that they go not only through the ear but through pores and cells into the ganglia, so that we hear not only aurally but with the whole being. We can counter sound with nonsound if we can devise ways to absorb it before it is heard or perceived. I would like to work on a Smotherer that will put out exactly matching negative waves to cancel out the positives before they travel into the receptor. Also, I'd like to play around with ultra-sound. Since it can literally shake dirt out of dry clothes, I feel certain that it can be directed to dislodge—eat up, if you will—tumors and unwanted fetuses and perhaps at certain modulations unpit acne, abrade tattoo marks, etc. It's a pity the human cochlea is such a poor machine."

❋ I FOUND OUT last night that Joe Ella is the kind of girl who needs no seducing to speak of. First we went to the movies, which consists of slathering yourself full of insect repellent and sitting on tarps on the grass in this bowl-shaped clearing and watching the moths attempt group suicide on the screen. It was *The African Queen,* by the way, a witty choice under the circumstances, and appropriately sweaty. Afterward we wandered off to the beach, Happy Fornicating Ground of thousands, and she told me this incredible story, one of her mother's case histories.

It seems there is this six-year-old child whose single parent is a whore. Since she is neither young nor pretty nor adroit, she works out of a one-bedroom apartment in a housing project and when her gentlemen callers come at night she takes the kid out of their one bed and locks him in a trunk in the kitchen. Sometimes he sleeps through the whole procedure, sometimes he wakes up and protests, whereupon she gives him his teddy and a cookie and pops him into his little coffin. Joe Ella feels that the logical solution to Binky's difficulties is to find a two-bedroom flat for his mother. This is what I mean by a research intellect. It is essentially a conservative approach, it keeps people at a distance by depersonalizing experience. I am very inept with Joe Ella, who is, however, good at giving directions in a detached, little-girl voice and calls her cunt "my cunny." This has the paradoxical effect of making me feel like a rapist and a very young boy all at once.

I confess I haven't had great varieties of experience fucking, which is simple enough for idiots to succeed at, but has a way of getting complicated the more I think about it. I am clumsy and false and exploitative just when I want to be most metaphysical. God knows, Cambridge and Manhattan were full of willing girls skulking about at parties in their Marimekko dresses. They were usually the kind who raised up on one elbow afterward and said, "Now tell me what you really think of my renovation design for East Tenth Street." Half of them lied about coming. There you are, you've just fucked this magnificent thing with wide, moony tits and gazelle legs that slithered all around your back and who's made all the appropriate appreciative sounds, whether or not they're dubbed in, how can you tell her her design is boring and repetitive and unimaginative? Whereas Joe Ella is small and compact and totally nononsense. She doesn't want sand in her crotch, she'll get the wrinkles out of the tarpaulin, she helps you with your belt like a practical nurse, she says, I'd like you to do this and this and when she comes she sings this very surprising thank you thank you thank you in your ear. I don't really want to be thanked. I mean, it isn't a courtesy gesture like holding a door open or handing her into a car and yet I can't get a grudging thank you yourself out of my mouth. This is going to take some figuring out.

✳ THE AID and HUD people flew in this week. One guy in particular strikes me. He's a Green Revolution fanatic, a plant geneticist. We spent a whole day on rust-resistant wheat and new strains of dry rice and how to double, sometimes triple the yield of a given region in one growing season, what he calls the LP factor, Living Proof. It seems there are two camps, something like the Jesuits and the Jansenists. The Jezzes are all for increasing world-food production with things like the Sudan grass-sorghum cross, and a rice strain that doesn't require cyclical flooding, and high-nutrition, low-cost foods like a powdered corn-soya-milk mix for child-feeding and energy-feeding programs. The Janzes want to grease the world with contraceptive jellies, put pills in the drinking water, give cash bonuses for vasectomies, etc. The Jezzes talk like the Janzes are a new breed of fascist, and the Janzes think the Jezzes are radico-pinko-Marxists and the irony is that they're all in this save-the-world thing together. I confess I am more inspired by the former than the latter. I am still simplistic enough to believe in economic amelioration, although I change sides like changing sheets. What I want is not to be on a side, but to serve. Of course there was a banquet, Boy Scout style, with awards and ceremonies and a lot of good-humored parodies in song and verse. Sort of like Thanksgiving dinner in an institution, heavy on the mashed potatoes and gravy and skimpy when it comes to carving from the breastbone.

Joe Ella and I conducted our farewells on the beach, but it wasn't all sandy and warm and bawdy as I would have hoped. She is so businesslike. We are probably destined never to see each other again. I think she is fated to fall in love with a behavioral scientist whose lifetime project will be to implant electrodes in monkey testicles to measure their testosterone pro-

duction when confronted with properly libidinous objects. She
will enthusiastically tabulate the results. Is this a way of saying
she made a monkey out of me? Good-by, Joe Ella. Thank you
thank you thank you. I really learned a lot.

✻ HELL WEEK, this furlough between the Caribbean and the
Ivory Coast. New York is hotter than St. Croix. The air stinks
of diesel fuel and the anger of sweaty people. The street noises
are overpowering. I feel like the air hammers are trepanning my
skull. I startle inside like a rabbit when the police or fire sirens
go past and once, at Columbus Circle when our taxi got caught
in a jam—about thirty demented drivers all leaning on their
horns together—I damn near burst out screaming. It took all
my will power to stay in the back seat, stay in the jangle. If this
is culture shock after only three months in a bland, American-
ized version of the tropics, with street lights and seven brands
of toothpaste, what will it be after two years in Africa? It's funny
how much I don't want to see old friends, don't want to be either
congratulated or commiserated with, want to keep this precarious balance, like an about-to-be seminarian. So I stick around
a lot with Dewey, who can go half a day without speaking. He
reads and I read and we put the Brandenburg concertos on loud
enough to sing over the air conditioner and let them repeat all
day. He is very controlled and at the same time very intense and
it's hard for him to eat. Whereas I have the appetite of a glutton.
Now I understand fat priests. Once I got him to go bowling but
he got so involved with figuring out the probability ratios of
strikes and spares that he filled up the whole score page with
mathematical doodles. The parents seem to have adjusted to
having him around. It's lovely and pathetic the way they cover
for him, adore him, accept him. Mother in particular, who

announces every evening at dinner, isn't this fun? Dewey, who may or may not be hallucinating at that point, looks at her as though he has never seen her before in his entire life, as in a way he has not. Dr. Sitzmark seems to have suggested that the best that can be hoped for is this bottled-up Dewey, who may or may not pull out of it, produce some incredible opus, add something to the physics of sound, a new theory of nonacoustics, or just go on having private visitations. He doesn't even pretend to understand him any more, just sees him twice a week, puts his fingertips together, asks him, any dreams? and nods and listens or just shares the silence. It's sad, but nothing I ever do in my life, in reality, will ever seem as heroic as Dewey's gentle madness.

❋ I LEAVE TONIGHT from Kennedy. London, Paris, then Air Afrique to Marseilles and Niger. Any dreams? Any prayers? One for the safekeeping of Dewey, to whom Elijah appeared this week for the second time. What they say to each other neither Sitzmark nor I is privileged to know, but I hope it is something old and wise and consoling, a vision of a better time maybe, a free place of the souls. Since it is Friday we had the candles and wine and the blessing, Mother lighting the tapers and Father very gravely filling the kiddush cup, a benign patriarch. Dewey most unexpectedly offered to sing Ayn Kelohaynu by way of a farewell to me, which he did flawlessly but in a young voice, his almost-soprano voice from the year he was bar mitzvahed, I recognized it. There was one tear like a little beach pebble on Mother's cheek, it sat there for the longest time and only fell when he finished singing, in time for her to declare *isn't this fun!* It's tearing me in two, the staying, the going.

❉ TO FIND THE COURAGE to begin to write in this journal again, when words have dropped away from me and I live each day by muscle and example and gesture. It's been a month now. English is funny in my mouth, a funny arrangement on the page. The scales fell from my eyes the night—actually two a.m.—our plane came down in Niamey in Niger, and we went into the long wooden shed that represents an airport to wait for our morning plane to Abidjan. Bare wooden benches, bare counters, bare light bulbs, and the eyes of the Third World on us hard as marble, the barest things of all. The air was like wet wool, nothing stirring. I alternately sweated and dried in salty rings and sweated wider rings and dried again. It's a sensation I'm used to now, comfortable in, but the sweat of St. Croix was as the polite glow of a warm maiden compared to this daily, funky, salt-crusted sweat. Men's mouths made sounds but they were shapeless, there was no meaning in anything, least of all in my presence there. My guts all turned to a watery shit churning around in me. I think I lived in a state of perpetual squeeze for about a week after. From Abidjan, Dominic Falco—The Falcon —and I came up to Maninian by jeep. At first there were paved roads, heavily forested on either side, mahogany mostly, and coffee plantations, which the French are still vigorously exploit- ing, and wood houses here and there. We drove for hours, my jaw ached from the jolting, then dirt roads, then mere tracks and meanwhile the lush vegetation thinning out and the world grow- ing drier and drier and hotter and hotter. Since our driver was a Moslem, we got five rest periods a day. At the appointed hour he simply cut the motor and we coasted to a stop—no need to pull over, no place really to pull over to—and he'd get out his little prayer rug and unpack his teapot to wash his hands and feet (never his face) and then he'd pray. The Falcon and I were embarrassed in about equal proportions, a half-Jesus, half-

Moses embarrassment, but it was something we soon got over. Just about everyone here is Moslem, a good religion for this treeless topography. It's a harsh life, parched and dusty during the dry season, and even crueler during the rains, when crops either prosper or get flooded out. The Moslem code stresses abstinence and honor and salvation. John Calvin would have been at home here.

❊ WE'RE TUCKED INTO the northwest corner of the IC, near the Guinea and Mali borders. Relationships with Guinea, which is considered to be very left-wing, are rather strained. I find myself thinking of Stokely Carmichael and wondering how he's getting on. Right now we're in the dry season. There isn't a cloud in the sky day after day, only an occasional dry lightning storm overhead, marvelous and fearful to watch, real Elijah pillars of lightning. The Falcon and I have a house of our own, just like everyone else's house, and we try to live right on the line according to the native style, except that we boil our water. The natives think the thicker the water, the more nutrients it has in it. Out of a Judaeo-Christian sense of body-shame, we've built a privy, really a glorified box, over our hole. Otherwise we conform pretty well and we are not overtly disliked. We've stopped thinking of accomplishments and rural animations—we just want to get along. Everyone is fascinated with the Falcon's hair, which on a girl would be called strawberry blond. It is immensely, fabulously curly. They come to touch it, cluck over it, ask for little wisps of it. I am dark enough now to hardly appear odd to them, or so I think. We announced the death of haircuts and thought about starting beards, but after three days of the stubble-itch, during which I imagined lice, gave up and recommended shaving.

❋ THE MAKING OF the bricks has turned into a real ceremony. We introduced the concept of the cement-block mold so that one man can now make two to three hundred bricks a day. This is much wondered at and exclaimed over. The villagers tend to skimp on cement, which is shipped up from Abidjan, so that many bricks crumble before they can be put in place, or you get this charming dumbshow of bricks being carried very tenderly like small babies to be put in place before they do crumble. I have thought of something to praise God for, from which He made the first man, also tenderly without cement or straw. It is called mud. We patch with mud, we trowel with mud, now that we have trowels, as marvelous to our workers as the spatula must have been to the first cook, and after *that* mud dries, we plaster with more mud. A mud house will last indefinitely if it is kept properly patched. The way they build their houses in a world without wood wipes out all Western notions of levels and squares and plumb bobs, and makes eminent sense. You begin with a piece of string half the diameter of the finished dwelling. You tie one end of this string to a stick and you firmly jab the stick into a previously flattened area. Then you draw a circle with your string and where the circle lies you dig a modest trench in which you lay the first course of bricks. And so on, up and up, in the circle that celebrates the sun, the roundness of the earth, the orange, God's stars, and His own fist. Mud is the plaster and the mortar, the smoother and the shaper. When your house is tall enough, it receives an umbrella of bamboo. You send for the specialist, the thatcher. There's one to every two or three villages. He takes the tall grasses and weaves them together to form a cone. This is skilled labor. To make a peak that doesn't leak or pull apart in the first rain is an art handed down from father to son. It is like getting into the plumbers' union. In a round house fifteen to twenty feet in diameter live one wife and her children. Since there are up to four wives, and a house of his own for the husband, and a cooking shed for rainy weather, each family forms a cluster of thatches around a central courtyard. If Dewey were here, he would diagram the six hundred-or-so clusters and discover a new element in the atomic table.

✳ A CHILD is missing today, barely a toddler, Fanta, third daughter of the well-digger, himself an unlucky third son, member of a tribal group that is looked down on because wells are so hard to dig in this stony soil that only a poor man takes up the trade. He spent the morning with a posse of five others looking for her, wandering around the outskirts of the village in a circle and hacking at the dry grass with his well-digger's hoe, but this afternoon he is back inside his hole, scraping it rounder and deeper. It is said that of course there will be no body. The Maninian, the enormous boa constrictor who has given his name to this village, has taken his periodic sacrifice. It is looked on as casually as a bride-price in a land where a log in the road can turn into a snake. Everyone seems rather relieved, as if they were thinking, well, *that's* over with for a finite time. This is exactly the kind of thing that was not covered in the PC lectures. We learned that the political system of the IC lies somewhere between a tutelary democracy and a modernizing oligarchy and that rates for infant mortality are unavailable, but we were never told, can a boa constrictor swallow a child?

✳ A BLEAK, sad, terribly sane letter from Dewey, who has burned up all his books and papers and theories in the living-room fireplace and, to keep from immolating himself with lighter fluid and sending the whole building up in flames, has committed himself to Eastgate for an indefinite stay. I feel sick in my gut thinking of him there two weeks now. He has spent so many years wandering around like a ghost in his childhood, always yearning backward with Dr. Sitzmark, the faithful St. Bernard, sniffing out his traumas like so many truffles to find what ones led to this "personality disorder" they've pinned on him. He has let the other part of his mind rummage forward, always hoping the intellectual excitement of discovery would save him, whether it was formulae and equations or dialogues with the vanished prophets. In another culture, say this IC one, he might have been a shaman, a holy man. In the good old U.S.A., where you conform to other people's realities or get pushed into the pit of despair, he is a schiz. "My pathology is not understood," he writes, "but the truth is that I am probably a very mediocre thinker after all. My delusions about negative sound and my apparitions of Elijah are not very different from the delusions of my neighbor here, who declares himself to be Christ." As of today after this heartbreak I *do* believe that a boa constrictor can swallow a child.

❋ WE ARE building a community building with wood shipped up from the coast. It is to be enclosed for use in the rainy season. This involves the magic of the white man's bubble, how it must be fitted into the middle of the little window before the boards can be nailed together. The concept of the right angle has come into our lives along with the tape measure. I am very humble about it. The original French colonials imposed a housing style on this country that was copied from the suburbs of Paris. They did not take into account the fact that you cannot funnel four wives through one European-style living room without creating enormous discord. I don't especially want to be a party to imposing a rectangular culture on a circular one, but we are going to show movies here and a screen requires a straight wall.

Resistance to this structure is very subtle, very real. For instance, if you live ninety-nine per cent of your life in the open, a window in a wall is a way for a thief to get in. Air and light and cross-ventilation are absurd considerations. Thus we design a window and receive a solid wall. The carpenters and masons pretend to be appalled. They are always very agreeable when you ask them to do something but they end up doing the diametric opposite of what they agreed to do. The reasoning is as circular as the architecture, but everyone's face is saved by it. Fuck windows, anyway. Why we are doing this remains unclear to me. The communists indoctrinate; the Americans corrupt. I am feeling better about Dewey. He sent me a chess move. The Falcon is helping me with a reply.

❋ SOMETIME THIS WEEK we celebrated a year here. The Falcon and I got privately drunk on a bottle of real Scotch that came up by way of the bush taxi. We've never seen a CARE shipment, except bits of stuff black-marketed for resale. But somebody down in Abidjan loves us. It was a terrible sodden experience, we both ended up crying about women. I am jealous of The Falcon, who has more of them to lament than seems humanly possible. I think that he's a terribly good liar. Summary of accomplishments at year's end:

How to cap wells to prevent contamination, and how to raise the water out with crank and pulley.
How to design housing around a central water supply.
How to improvise a bridge that won't wash out in the rainy season. How to live through the rainy season.
How to patch the flat tire of a Mobilette in a downpour with latex from the nearest rubber tree.

How to tell the deadly green mumba snake from its harmless cousins.

How to grow dry rice and plant an orange grove. How to keep goats out of same. How to eat goat and keep it down.

How to sing the "Abidjanaise," which is the national anthem. How to speak a little Djula and how to write it in the romance alphabet.

How to be celibate, though not how not to burn.

How to love thine own masochism.

❋ DEWEY IS DEAD. He killed himself. I am writing this in Abidjan, waiting for a plane out. I am to have thirty days compassionate leave. Damn Sitzmark. Damn psychiatry. Damn the parents. Damn this whole asshole world that couldn't save him. And damn you, Dewey, for dying on me behind my back.

❋ THE LIGHT HAD BEGUN to fall from the sky when Robin finished reading. It was cold. She sat on the loose pages to keep them from flying away and she let the harbor stench blow on her face while she waited for her feelings to sift out and settle. Jeff's concerns were not all *me me* concerns, like hers. It was a good thing that she had cut the cord between them. It was a good thing that Gran and Tante were on the water. It was a good thing that she alone was beached high and dry. If she sat here alone much longer it would be dark enough to get mugged. That was not part of the creative experiment; that was not part of coming into her own. She packed up her papers and smoothed out her skirt and started back briskly across the campus. The street lights were just coming on. She walked behind people and crossed at corners and went down into the subway. She was a part of the general purpose.

8

ExtraVagance

THE FIRST SOUND Robin heard the day she came back alone to Little Mink Hill was the bleating of the vealers. A pair of swallows had nested in New Jersey's lean-to. Chipmunks were busy in what remained of last winter's woodpile. She dawdled there, floating, her bones grown light as milkweed puffs as in a sudden moment of *déjà vu*. She could not cope with that sudden rush of feeling. Either time would stop and the moment freeze like an ice sculpture, or it would plunge headlong down the slope and be lost forever.

The house took the noon sun on its front windows like a woman sunbathing, eyes closed. There was nothing to read on that face and yet she had not expected a text to be apparent there. She might put her arms against the wood, pick with her thumb the splinters a year's weathering had raised, tell the shingles aloud, Hello House, but it could give nothing back. She had stood shoulder to shoulder with Jeff to build it and had lived in it with him through the turning of three seasons. What she could not yet do was to be her own survivor. Was it something she had ever known? Must we repeat what we do not remember? She had come back to render obsolete the stale scenes of the year that stood behind her. Nevertheless, they were vivid, scudding across her retina; Axel, glittering in Zurich with the stolen jewels. Her china-doll mother, Beth, in the arms of nurse Gloria. Gran's dowager hump month by month taking her head down angrily like a turtle's.

Muhner saved her, hallooing from the barn and coming toward her. Albert Muhner, red-faced and red-armed with his neatly rolled-up sleeves. They went together to inspect the garden Jeff had put in before leaving for Outward Bound training school. She thought of Jeff devising fish traps and scaling cliffs in British Columbia. Jeff teaching kids to challenge their forgotten pioneer instincts. How to navigate by compass and topological map, how to survive in isolation in the woods. How to spend the night with your back to a tree, how to nurse a four-day fire with two kitchen matches. Meanwhile she would settle in to establish her own Outward Bound. She would back against her own tree, however spindly or tame.

The corn was up, shin high. When she saw how the garden had been laid out with two rows of woodchuck corn all around the perimeter and these backed by a single line of marigold plants, Robin said, "It's like tithing in a way. Holier, really."

"Soil's too heavy for good corn anyways," Muhner explained. "But anything the chucks leave, the marigolds'll keep the bugs off. Now Robin, you come over to the barn. I got something for you."

Something was a puppy, a golden retriever with absurdly big paws and a fernlike tail. Of course she should have known! Tears stood in her eyes; friendship made her clumsy.

"One thing, though. He ain't house-trained," Muhner warned. "You got to watch him good for ticks, too."

She was embarrassed to be snuggling the puppy so readily. He squirmed free and began worrying a stick. "What's his name?"

"That's for you to decide."

"Dusty," she said.

Privately his name was Dostoevsky. That evening he ate so hugely and hungrily that his belly swelled and she was alarmed at the hot round drum it formed. There was milky oatmeal on his nose and his front paws. He waddled serenely to the middle of the room and puddled there, meanwhile yawning. Puddled in her one little room. "We always imagine eternity as something vast, vast!" Svidrigailov had told Raskolnikov. "What if it's one little room, like a bathhouse in the country, black and grimy and spiders in the corner, and that's all eternity is?"

"One does not pee inside eternity," she told the puppy, and took him outside in the early dark, where he batted at moths and ate a buttercup.

He also chased chickens, dug holes in the garden, and with great industry chewed all the chair legs.

He could not bear to be left behind, so that she took him to town to the general store. On the end of a much too stout rope he fell asleep on Robin's sneaker.

"Is he all right, your puppy?" A woman on crutches was leaning toward her. She had strong sunburned arms and a handsome face with crescent smile creases. Her left leg was in a cast which had been fancifully decorated with Magic Markers. "I know I've seen you in here before—was it last summer?"

"He just does that," Robin said. "When he's tired enough he just goes to sleep anywhere." She had been idling, reading the soup-can labels so as to avoid any with meat stock.

The woman's name was Erica Morton. Her husband was a surgeon and was still in the city, which meant Manhattan. They had a house on the back and fashionable side of Big Mink Hill, a mile from Robin over the ridge by footpath, four miles by public road. She had broken her leg when her horse refused a fence. And this was her house guest, David Despery, presently on the lam from TV programing. "He's cleaning the Augean stables," she explained. "The kids aren't too great with a pitchfork."

"It's a real switch from screening talk-show contestants," he told her. "Ten years of Today and Midday and Tonight prima donnas with autobiographies to peddle. I cut out. I decided it was time for Tomorrow."

Robin decided that she disliked him. Too quick to establish a beachhead, announce his qualifications. Still, he was amiable to look at, listen to. Tall, thirty-fivish, sandy, skinny, an agreeably flat speech that suggested the Middle West.

"How many horses do you have?"

"Two real ones and an overweight pony," Erica said. "Still, it adds up to a lot of horseshit."

"Do you ride?" David asked her.

"I haven't, for years. I used to love it when I was little."

"Now you're big," he said.

It was provocative. "Now I'm big," she agreed.

"David would love someone to ride with," Erica said. "Why don't we get better acquainted? Come over for drinks and supper."

"Better than that," David offered. "I'll ride over and get you around five. I can tie William behind."

"Oh, yes!" Erica was enthusiastic. "We can run you back later by road."

"I'm a vegetarian," Robin announced. "And I can't leave Dusty alone."

"That can all be accommodated," he said.

❋ THREE DAYS LATER he kissed her. They had tied the horses at the edge of woodlands that had once been pasture. The yellow warblers called a witchety, witchety! alarm on all sides and flew up from their browsing like so many tame canaries. Robin tramped round a thicket full of high bush berries. They were hard green still, in immense clusters. "The birds'll get them," she said. "You'll see. Day by day they'll clean off the ripe ones."

"An orgy," he agreed. She knew berries were not on his mind. And not the daisies, or the furry honeybees that walked heavily in their centers. She knew he did not see that they had come too late for the woods strawberries, just beginning to die back among the scarlet leads that had signaled the birds. He bent down to make it easy for her to kiss him back and she closed her eyes and swam into the moment. Everybody is weak, she told herself.

She guessed he had been Erica's lover and it had come to this kind of *détente.*

It was all happening too fast; she was dizzy with it. They sat under an oak tree, a little removed from the hum and buzz of the invaded field. Last year's acorn bits were crumbling to humus under her fingers.

"Not here," she said.

"Robin. There isn't anyone around for miles."

"I don't want to. Okay?"

"Okay." But getting up he held out a hand to her and she came not unwillingly into his arms again. "Some other time," he said, into her hair.

She said nothing, even knowing her silence was an act of consent.

They cantered most of the way back. She had graduated from William, the overweight pony, to Erica's own mare. She concentrated on the business at hand; sinking back a little in the saddle to keep a good seat, thrusting down with her heels. Toes in, she reminded herself. Knees snug, et cetera.

She could see inchworms hanging down from the alders, and the threads of this morning's spider webs as she broke through, ducking overhanging branches.

Whereas David rose easily, with the assurance of a seasoned horseman. He was at home with animals in the same way that he might have been at home with cars. He was not sentimental about horses, the vealers were a perfectly natural phenomenon, the puppy was old enough to be shut up alone for a few hours, and the best way to get rid of the marauding woodchucks was with a .22. A service he'd be glad to perform, if she liked.

On the contrary, she was prepared to sacrifice all the corn. Let them have the carrots, too, for that matter. She was no killer. The splay of dead nestlings on the path, flatter than the gingerbread man, suggested to her fetal shapes. No matter that nature was doing its own careless weeding. She would not be a contributor.

All this she tried to convey to David, who listened with an edge of what she took to be contempt. There was a tiny capillary etched in the corner of his right eye; it betrayed him. It was the Delta of his inner Mississippi, a frail blood path against the hard bright white. At the corners of his mouth lines moved and changed their surfaces with his mood. They would one day be crevices.

The flat speech pattern that she took for Middle West had originated in Tennessee, with all the Southern honed out of it. He was the son of a dirt farmer, his genius and his Board scores discovered by an ardent spinster English teacher who had heard of Yale. She was determined he would go there. Accordingly, they applied for scholarships. The college granted him tuition and a loan against room and board. Miss Jeffers thought to apprise Harvard of his situation; he went north for interviews. Harvard countered with his full costs underwritten. Hasty Pudding performed his shows two years running and after graduation he fell quite naturally into the television industry, at first hosting a breakfast show, then serving a stint at news casting, the wrap-up after the late movies. There was a marriage coterminous with his next post, but no children. His wife had been of course a Personality. He did not believe in marriage, *en principe*, for creative people. He felt that total love was to be resisted, along with all other total immersions, church or state. He was a Detached Man. Of all this she stood forewarned.

She had her own demurrers. Hadn't she observed a generation of wives who served as donkey engines, hoisting and pulling? Didn't she know that women lose the rights to their bodies under the marriage contract? Shouldn't feminists direct their attention to the abolition of marriage as an institution for legal slavery? Wasn't it a typical smokescreen to claim that marriage could be based on love? Love means different things to different people. Indeed, were there any happy marriages? It was a question he might have asked as well as she. Still, asking it singled out the escapees from society. And she was one of them, squatting, weeding down the garden row where Jeffrey Rabinowitz's bush beans and green onions alternated in a companionate planting. David watched.

"Companionate means they're inhospitable to each other's natural pests," she explained.

"Organic?" he asked.

"Long before organic got to be a word. Why, even Thomas Jefferson did it. Damn!" She straightened, swatting at a mosquito that had bitten through her raised rump. "Little bastards, they bite right through the cloth. You wonder how they manage."

That mosquito was a connoisseur, he told her.

Unaccountably, she thought of Tante's sunken buttocks that had once been little plump cushions. To distract herself she told him, "Jefferson said something awfully nice, once. It's humble, that's why I like it. 'But though I am an old man, I am but a young gardener.' "

"Jefferson, hey? Not Thoreau this time. What a little quote monger you are. You know what? Your head is a bank vault stuffed full of useless aphorisms."

She scratched, considering this, then let it pass.

"I'm not putting you down," he said. "It's endearing."

"Yes you were. But it's true, in a way. I read things and then I make them mine. They fit into me."

"And you pop them into the proper metal box."

"But I don't lock them in. They belong to anybody who wants them."

"Well, supposing I want this one, the Jefferson thing. What does it mean with all those buts?"

" 'But though I am an old man, I am but a young gardener?' That he was young in every garden, they were new together. Also meaning, no matter how many years he gardened, he would still be only a beginner in the span of growing time."

"We're all beginners," he said in his kind, neutral tone. But she could see that it didn't really touch him. "Come on, get up from your Protestant work ethic and let's go have a guilty bloody mary."

She dusted herself off vigorously. "Why guilty? I've earned mine."

"Well, I haven't. So you can share my guilt."

"You," she whispered at his retreating back, "haven't felt a twinge of guilt since you popped out of the womb. That's the beauty of you."

❊ "I AM FALLING into a love affair with David Despery," Robin wrote in her journal that night with the puppy whimpering asleep in his box on the hearth, "the way Jeff fell into the Peace Corps."

. . . It is ironic. Perhaps what I am doing is avenging myself for Joe Ella, although how can you avenge something that took place in other people's pasts before you even met them? I'm having my own kind of holy war here. First of all, I don't believe in what I'm doing (encouraging him), then I hate myself for not being true to first principles (know thyself), then my body speaks up and I feel deliciously juicy. And then I turn terribly sardonic, thinking what the hell, you only get one trip through life (*sardonius risus,* the death smile.) I read somewhere that the death-smile idea came from a favorite poisonous plant used to commit suicide. It distorted the face of the eater. I think of a self-portrait done by Barbara Swan, the Boston artist, that I saw last month in a Newbury Street gallery. I was between Tante's and Gran's when I looked up and saw it from the street and I had to go inside for a closer look. She has painted her face and figure within a frame and inside the frame there is the outline of a looking glass, one of those immense, tilted old-fashioned pier glasses. She is holding a bottle in her hands, raising it up to the light. The blue of the old bottle is reflected in one of her eyeglass lenses. The other, the seeing eye, so to speak, remains clear. On the table in front of her in the painting there is another bottle. It takes and refracts the red pattern of her dress. The bottle on the table stands outside the mirror and so is painted twice, from the outside and the inside. It is endlessly fascinating to me because it is so many ways of seeing. Through a glass darkly, and face to face. My relationship with David is like that, too. He is a man of many parts, some of them refractable.

❉ DAVID SAYS a gardener is someone who has been blocked in the area of developing normal human relationships, and moralizes by way of a garden. He also says it is a badge of my caste, like having a charge account at the Snooty Fox (I don't) or belonging to the country club (Gran does, but she never goes). He and Erica have discussed this at length. Erica, who is very breezy and modern on the surface and whom I am prepared to like very much but in my own wary way, is possibly speaking through David. Or does he make these kinds of Freudian value judgments on his own? Although he himself is a terrible snob. It's a result of being up from what he describes as red-neck poverty. So when he mocks the growing of things you eat as an unnecessary exercise in bedding and marshaling and controlling, I know it is just an inevitable reaction against his childhood. There was a time when he worked eight hours a day drowning potato bugs in kerosene. Now he is a man of a hundred credit cards. He says there is nothing he does that he cannot defer payment on. Coast to coast. We will see about that.

❉ DAVID TALKS A LOT about the sacrosanct idleness of the well-to-do. Meaning not only me, but Erica as well. I am *sure* now that they were lovers. She has a way of possessing him from across the room that makes me think of Laura's sidelongs. He does not understand at all about the enforced rigor. The starchiness that comes along with privilege and does not give way to shiftlessness, but to schemes for self-improvement. For instance, next week Erica's Fresh Air Fund children will arrive. She calls them, in an excess of self-disgust, her pickaninnies. I am not sure David catches the extra edge of the irony; for him, they will *be* pickaninnies plain and proper. Her own two little ones she refers to as her biological children. Jennifer is not too bratty, although I think a ten-year-old ought not to whine so much. There are times for whining, and then there are times for bearing up. Jennifer hasn't gotten around to the bearing up part yet. And Brian is mostly impossible. I am trying to remember whether other eight-year-old boys hit and kick that much. It is known technically as sibling rivalry. As an only child I know nothing about sibling rivalry except at a safe remove, and far too little about the Oedipus complex (Erica's other touchstone), having had a father so briefly.

❋ I AM MAKING bread for David. Sesame egg twist, a dirty trick. I can see what is coming next. He is a most attractive man with a long jaw and rather a stern mouth. I am not particularly in love with him, but constancy does not seem to be my nature. The longer I live alone the less I like myself. Or at least the self I'm living with here. Today I picked the first baby string beans and dug out a dozen beets. They are the size of marbles but they bleed in my kitchen like the Sacred Heart. Dusty is half house-broken. That is, he makes his Number Twos (hideous old-maid terminology) out behind New Jersey's shed. There is a cemetery of little golden-retriever turds there.

❋ WHAT WAS COMING next has happened. We did it out there in the same field, the one I want to go back to some day when the strawberries, the sow's teats strawberries are ripe, some other season. The horses calmly browsed. I couldn't, it seemed, do it here. Certainly not at Erica's, I am not liberated enough for that. I have discovered that coming with him is a matter of mechanics. I don't feel anything like Columbus. Really what I feel are two things. One is: mildly smug. Even while the heart may think it has been contravened, the body carries on. The other is: rockily out of sorts. I don't like this new truth. *It isn't nice,* the firm, arbitrary, totally unreasonable judgment Gran used to pass on a thousand things. It isn't nice to sit like that, it isn't nice to stare at deformed people, it isn't nice to blow your nose on toilet paper. These, I realize, were all in the area of manners, and I mean something far more than that. It was different with Jeff, who made conversation while we made love. We were attached. Whatever rucked up or rakish way our bodies went, we belonged to each other. David, on the other hand, is far away. Tante, who went on stag-and-boar hunts in her childhood, used to say, Of course now one goes to the zoo. Or reads dreadful books about loving a lion or bringing up chimpanzees in your apartment. There is a connection. It is the difference between participating and performing.

❋ I WEEDED ALL MORNING and considered it a penance. Weeding in a way corrupts the gardener. There were purslane and sorrel and poke. These are decreed to be weeds because Jeff didn't plant them. But nature does her own sowing. How do I dogmatically classify this as a vegetable, that as a weed? Salsify, Jerusalem artichoke, dock, all those things gone wild that were once cultivated. Escaped from gardens, the botanists say. I see them on their hands and knees along roadsides and in pastures patiently coaxing seeds from the flower heads so they can grow them properly in beds again. Like tansy, which used to be a proper British bloom and now runs wild everywhere. Me too. Only I do my escaping on the inside. Thoreau says it. *Extra vagance!* it depends on how you are yarded.

✿ THE FRESH AIR PIX have come. I went to Erica's this afternoon as promised and took Dusty to be patted and squeezed half to death. They are very shy little kids, there is so much to be scared of. The horses seem enormous and threatening to them. Big as dinosaurs, feet like dinner plates. We went swimming, but Dwayne is the shivery pretzel kind of little boy who is terrified of drowning. His bones are small but they outweigh him and the more he thrashes about, the faster he sinks. Shirley, who is older and chubby besides, managed better. At eleven she is already sprouting breasts. Erica says tonight will be the hardest time. They will be homesick for the streets and frightened of the night noises and the boy will wet his bed. This is her third summer of the Fresh Air Fund, so she speaks with authority. Erica means to be kind but it comes off all too often as flippant. I didn't want to confuse things by staying any later. David was visibly annoyed. He wanted to come back here with me but I pointed out that Erica needed him. She is pretty depressed herself. The leg itches fantastically under the cast in this heat. Never having broken anything of his own, David doesn't understand this. She stumps around on her crutches till her arms ache. They quarreled like man and wife. I suppose he has told her about the other day, voyeurism being her only pleasure at the present. It might have gone something like this:

By the way, I made it with your little friend day before yesterday, did I tell you?

Robin, you mean? The little girl in the shack?

Come off it, darling. What other little friend?

Congratulations.

Aren't you going to ask me how it went?

Why? Was it amusing? Did she invite you to bugger her?

Christ no! It was very old-fashioned. Missionary position. Under a tree in a very scratchy field, in fact.

Poor David.

It seems she has all these scruples about her bed. Or for that matter, any of yours.

Too bad, baby. That's your problem.

I wouldn't have told you if I'd known it was going to irritate you.

I'm not irritated. I'm just not running a charity commune here.

Course you are, darling. You planned it all out in advance, didn't you?

Don't be nasty to me, David. I feel rotten.

Want a back rub?

Now they have rubbed each other down to a kind of warring friendship.

❋ IT RAINED all day. Erica and I drove over to New London with all four kids. We had lunch at the inn, I can't think why —for the edification or intimidation of the Pix? To give the blue-haired ladies of New London the finger? Or to display Erica Morton as Lady Bountiful? Erica claimed it was so we could have a civilized cocktail in a dry place (their living-room cathedral ceiling is leaking a tiny bit in one corner) and also so that David could have a day off from his labors. Once he mucks out the manure, that is. Eating out doesn't faze the Morton offspring. The minute the menus came Jennifer told everybody that Salisbury steak was just a dress-up name for hamburger.

Brian wanted to know where the lobster was, what kind of a restaurant didn't have lobster. Dwayne on the other hand said he didn't want no spoon, didn't the lady know he didn't drink no goddam coffee. And poor Shirley just sat there looking ready to cry. Everybody was ravenous and surly by the time the food came. Afterward, to appease them, we went to the fake-quaint general store and Erica let the kids buy tons of penny candy. They squabbled about dividing it all the way home. It was still raining, so for an extra treat they were packed off to play in the hayloft, which is absolutely ruinous for the hay. It threshes the seeds out of the heads. We three adults, if that's what we are, built a roaring fire and drank Vouvray and played Scrabble. David is very good at this. He is a purist and will not allow *et, ux,* or *ad,* which made Erica sulky. Of course he won, and with a phenomenally high score. I fed the kids tomato soup and cheese sandwiches for their supper and David took them all upstairs to supervise their baths. As soon as they had gone Erica said in a very calm way, "Isn't it incredible. Now I am exactly the kind of woman I hated and feared all my life. A matron, crowding forty. Holding up all the complicated underpinnings of these disorderly little lives."

I said I found it hard to think of her as middle-aged, whatever that means. Middle age gets older, the older you get. For instance, I choke over the phrase young adult. I am still trying to unlock the door and pry the child out.

Nevertheless, Erica said. She was middle-aged. And so was David, or he would be any minute. Because she couldn't do any of this without him. "We are like mother and father with our own Fresh Air Fund," she said, waving one hand around to where the leak pinged into a bucket and bits of Brian's Erector Set lay scattered.

And thus she claimed him.

I said I couldn't see where young adult melts into middle age, or how you put your seasons together.

She said that I would find out in due time and, moreover, it was no good trying to pry the child loose because a little dwarf sits inside all of us and we are all corrupted. And she for one detested having to put up with hers while at the same time playing mother to the world.

It was on the tip of my tongue to ask her why she did it, then, adding the Fresh Air Pix to her own biologicals. She suddenly said, "I've had two breakdowns already, you know. I might be on the verge of another."

I said that didn't seem at all likely to me. I thought of her as the soul of mental health and blah blah, or did she mean post-partum depressions because if so . . . This kind of intimacy makes me nervous and I tend to talk a lot in the spaces.

That wasn't at all what she meant. On the contrary, she simply had to keep on having kids, her own or others. Or a parade of lovers, it all came down to the same thing, it gave her some centrality, she needed to be needed and adored. Otherwise, she was sawdust.

We had been sitting a bit uncomfortably on the couch talking side by side to each other. I got up and stood in front of the fireplace so I could see her better. I wanted to ask her why she had handed David over to me, but then thought better of it. Maybe she had and maybe she hadn't.

When David brought me back here, I meant to ask him but we became otherwise involved.

❋ LETTERS TODAY from Gran and Tante. They complain about each other in the manner of old lovers. Tante says that the crossing was "bracing" and there was never a day that she did not take several turns on deck. Gran claims that the ship was hideously mismanaged, they were forced to ride out a storm at half speed, the captain deliberately taking the swells broadside. As a result she has been able to keep down only bouillon and dry toast "whereas Tessa displayed a remarkable gluttony." They are lying over a week in Copenhagen; Tante finds it an exhilarating city, "but your grandmother faults the service and the plumbing." Gran grudges it a certain charm but claims that the central plaza "is overrun with ill-mannered young Americans flaunting their unwashed long hair. Moreover, Tessa insists on speaking German to any and all who will listen." By the time I finished reading their letters I felt positively maternal. Each child having told me her side of things, as it were. Went riding again. David is teaching me how to jump. Still no letter from Jeff.

❋ RAINING AGAIN, almost a week straight now. It will be good for the mushrooms though not much else. Erica got a baby-sitter and she and David drove over for supper. Erica crutched round and round admiring the house. I must admit I enjoyed showing it off. In celebration I splurged and pulled nine very baby squashes. The garden will probably all rot, anyhow. We had a vegetarian feast, not one thing store-bought except the cupboard staples. They had of course never eaten wild lily buds before. I flourished playing housewife, David said it was positively unbecoming. Erica and I talked about what it means, being for the people, the common man, the oppressed minorities. David said that the nature nuts, the Sierra clubbies etc., run away from the masses. They want to keep the wild lands wild for their own uses, segregate themselves, the backpackers, from the asphalters. He was preaching at me. He also said that the reason ecologists lean toward the imminent apocalypse theory is that it's an acceptable way of expressing their hatred for people. He can be sensationally intellectually nasty. To mollify, Erica told the story of how she broke her leg. She says that while she was flying through the air she saw David hunched deep in the saddle, watching her with the most horrified expression on his face. That's when she knew she was going to break something. She thinks psychologically that she gave up and let it happen. The night her cast was put on, David sat up with her and held her toes to prove they were still there. "She was sure they'd been amputated," David said. "The only way she knew they were still attached was if I held them for her." Erica said she was afraid they would break off one by one and roll around the floor like lost marbles. It was getting more and more heroic the way they told it. When it was time for them to go home, we all stood in the doorway hugging and kissing, with the puppy getting tangled up in all the legs and crutches. Dusty is just like me, he wants to belong to everyone. It has left me with an eerie feeling. As though Erica and David and I are a *ménage à trois*.

❋ RACCOONS GOT into the corn last night. Greedy little beggars, they've stripped every ear I was hoarding and gloating over. I could have cried, except it was funny, too. As though I'd hoed and trenched for weeks just for them, one giant banquet for Racky Raccoon and his nineteen hooded cousins. You can see the trails of husks clear down to the pond, where they went to wash them. This is what comes of setting yourself over and against nature. Muhner has offered me his transistor radio. I am to leave it in the garden, tuned high to rock and roll all night. It seems there is an all-night station for raccoons. If Jeff were here he would remind me that in the Talmud a man is forbidden to eat before he feeds his animals. Well, now they are overfed. Three letters from him today, written a week apart but mailed in a bunch. One is advice about the corn (too late). One is about his students' projects. For instance, one boy is boring holes and taking the temperature of trees to see which are hotter, deciduous or evergreen. Another is pickling reindeer moss and some-one else has built a netting trap in which he caught a saw-whet owl. I would hate to have to eat an owl. And the last, written after he got mine, is about how to housebreak a puppy. Speaking of which, if Dusty weren't such a coward I could leave him tied up all night outside the garden. Which would kill two birds with one stone since there is still a puddle under the stove every morning.

❊ MY GOD, the tomatoes! They have come ripe all at once the last three days in the heat wave. I have given Erica thousands, and the Fresh Air Pix took a bagful home to the city. Muhner says I must can the rest. He has brought me his canning kettle and instructions. Gran and Tante come home Sunday.

❊ WEIRD WEEKEND. Erica's husband has arrived for his vaca-tion. They insisted we must all go to New London for an elegant dinner the first night. Stanley still in a business suit, a small square man with gray hair. Very distinguished but with a wet mouth. He toes out when he walks, like a man who is not used to exercise. Erica was not herself. Coquettish with both men. Also, her earrings were enormous. I was still stained all pinkish from having blanched, peeled, and processed twenty quarts of tomatoes. David flashing credit cards was a vulgarian. Everyone had too much to drink, including me. End of the story was that

David spent the night in my bed and I spent the night in my sleeping bag in front of the fireplace listening to the terrible engine of his sleep. Since this is never going to happen again, I really don't care that he snores. What I do care about is that I feel tricked by the two of them, David and Erica, who made me a part of their extended family and then used me to deceive Stanley with. Although I can't believe that Stanley was ever deceived. Probably they play these kinds of games over and over. I shouldn't say that I feel tricked, either, because I knew it all along and I enjoyed it well enough. It is a vain ambition to know thyself because thy selves keep changing.

✳ THIS MORNING I went to town to call first Gran, then Tante. This is how it went: They were hours on the pier and most rudely ushered through by the customs men (Gran). The fiords of Norway defy my poor English vocabulary, Binnie (Tante). Of course traveling with Tessa becomes wearisome, she is so childish in her enthusiasms (Gran). I refused to let your grandmother sully the trip for me with her cynical attitude (Tante). I promised to come down over next weekend. Bless you, my children. You are safely returned.

✳ GRAN HAS HAD a heart attack and is in the M.G.H. Tante called and bewildered poor Muhner by asking for Betty. He ran down in his underwear to get me. He had just finished up in the barn for the afternoon and was about to take a bath. I am taking the evening bus. It leaves in half an hour.

9

In Houses of Pearl and Porcelain

THE HOSPITAL lobby was hotel-like. People, laughter, potted plants, Coke machines. Except for a squawk box intermittently paging various doctors, Robin thought she might have been at an M.L.A. meeting. She inquired at the desk and was directed to the Intensive Care Unit, fourth floor.

The elevator smelled of ether and Pinesol. At the nurses' station a large, tired-face woman wearing on her left breast a pin that said MRS. CARTER was doing a crossword puzzle. She explained, "All heart patients are placed in Intensive Care for the first forty-eight hours. It's a routine procedure."

"But when can I see her?"

"No visitors after seven P.M. And only members of the immediate family. One at a time, for ten minutes. Are you a member of the immediate family?"

"I am the *only* immediate family," Robin said.

Mrs. Carter abandoned her crossword puzzle and heavily, wearily, as if pushed beyond her endurance, selected a file folder from the revolving stack.

"Lydia Latham. It says here, a surviving daughter. You're not her daughter?"

"Her daughter is my mother. My mother is . . . out of town, she's not well herself."

Mrs. Carter closed the folder and slipped it back in position. "I'm sorry. If you were her daughter I could make a tiny exception. You'll have to come back tomorrow. Not before noon."

"Tomorrow! But she's on the Danger List, she might be dead by tomorrow!"

"You must never say things like that," the nurse said angrily. "Never, never! Everyone in Intensive Care is placed on the Danger List. It's a routine procedure."

You must never. That was a splinter in the entrails, pricking its old familiar litany in the dark. "Look. Can I at least leave her a note or something? So when she wakes up tomorrow she can read it and know that I've come?"

"You can leave her a note all right," Mrs. Carter said coldly. "The nurse on duty will have to read it to her. Patients in Intensive Care may not have their eyeglasses. They are not permitted to read or write. No dentures or jewelry or watches. They remain under sedation for forty-eight hours."

Robin moaned.

Mrs. Carter inspected her. "Where is your mother? When is she coming?"

"My mother is an alcoholic. She's in a sanatorium in Lake Placid, I don't even know if she'll be allowed to come."

"Do you want me to break all the rules? Do you want me to jeopardize my position?"

Robin, ashamed, nodded.

Mrs. Carter heaved herself up and came out from behind the partition. "Come on, then," she said briskly. "But you better behave yourself."

"What does that mean, behave myself?"

"No tears. No hysterics."

"I wasn't planning to."

"People don't plan. They just do it."

Thus admonished, Robin tiptoed down the corridor behind the nurse's bulk.

Her grandmother was in a closet. A bellyband held her in place on the bed. A tube was taped to her nose. Another ran from under the sheets to a plastic bag that was fastened to the bed. Other wires conveyed her heartbeat to a screen across which the actions of her heart made bright little blips. Glucose dripped into a vein in her wrist. Her eyes were slitted open but she made no sign of recognition.

"Gran?" Robin whispered. "It's me, it's Binnie."

The body in the bed sighed a small wispy sigh. A little dribble of saliva appeared at one corner of its mouth.

"She is heavily sedated," Mrs. Carter remarked in a normal tone of voice. To Robin it sounded like a shout.

"Gran?" she whispered again.

Mrs. Carter crossed to the bed and pumped the body's free arm. "Mrs. Latham?" she roared. "Wake up, Mrs. Latham. Your granddaughter is here."

One eye opened to reveal a dilated pupil, then half closed itself again. *I don't know you,* it said.

"What are . . . all these?" Robin hissed.

"The nasal tube is for oxygen," Mrs. Carter boomed. "Easier to breathe. That," she gestured, "is an in-dwelling catheter. It's a routine procedure in Intensive Care. And of course we're monitoring her heart action. It's closed-circuit television, I can sit at the station and see all four screens at once."

"Is her . . . heart action very bad?"

"I've seen worse," Mrs. Carter said guardedly. "The period

of highest risk is the first forty-eight hours. If there's going to be a second attack."

"If there is, what will you do?"

"Resuscitate," Mrs. Carter said firmly. "We have all the heroic measures available here in Intensive Care."

Robin sat by the bed for several minutes waiting for a sign. This was the Mother-Father of her being, this rag body tied down in the bed. This had fed and clothed her, admonished and, strictly speaking, loved her into adulthood. So much was a matter of empty hands, of accident. You did what was expected of you. Learning to tie your shoelaces, keeping up appearances. Courtesy to relatives, alms to the poor. Without any male model, serving your apprenticeship in a world of men and women. You are born strong. Without dictionary or alphabet you learn about death.

Going out, Robin said, "Thank you," but Mrs. Carter was resettled with her crossword puzzle or chose not to hear. After all, she had broken the rules.

Toward morning, the blips that crossed the screen faltered and grew more erratic. The heroic measures were resorted to and then abandoned. Before the sun came up, Gran died.

For a long time Robin felt numb. It was so awful not having said good-by. Her grandmother, who had staked her lifetime on observing the proprieties, would have taken it hard, her not saying good-by that way. Although she had tried, she had called to her and not been recognized. No, that was ridiculous, in death there are no proprieties. No little farewell luncheons, no flowers or candy boxes, no *bon voyages.* You simply go out without so much as a wave. Still, everything felt so unfinished. Left over. On the coffee table in front of her, a pile of her grandmother's effects. They had been taken from the hospital safe when the last heroic measures failed. Two rings. A gold bracelet lavished with seed pearls. The brooch she was seldom without. A diamond watch. And a steel-gray, human-hair, hand-sewn-in-Italy wig.

Tante found consolation in going over and over the details.

"In Bonwit Teller, mind you, Binnie. Where not a single salesperson recognized her. You know how your grandmother felt about Bonwit Teller. She swore she would never cross the threshold, she could never forgive the powers that be for abandoning the Museum of Natural History."

"I know," Robin said, for whom it had always been Bonwit's, a severe stone building set back from the street, with the kind of showcase windows that are called understated.

"She loved that museum, no matter how dingy it was. When I think how those floorboards tilted and creaked. You had the sense that they might give way at any moment. The whole place smelled of mothballs, and no wonder. Dozens of tawdry stuffed creatures behind glass, and such tiny printed labels. You had to squint to read them. The worst of them all was that gorilla done up with an awful forced grin. And the lips painted red. Red! *I* never understood what your grandmother found of interest there. Except that it was Old Boston, you know. A sense of belonging, you know how much that meant to her."

"In the Better Dress Department," Robin coached, anxious to get the story over with.

"In the Better Dress Department. She was looking for a serviceable wool, she said to me that morning that she meant to put her fall wardrobe in order early, while there were still some sensible choices. She had this notion, Binnie, that by Labor Day there would be nothing left in wool except pinks and blues. She wanted something in burgundy, or failing that, grape. 'Black is unremitting, Tessa,' she said to me. 'I am not in mourning for the world.' Those were the last words she spoke to me."

They were both silent. Robin, fearing the pause would give way to tears (had she ever seen Tante cry?), rushed to fill the gap. "But she always said black was essential. Black was—what did she call it?—the mainstay of the mature woman."

"I think it was the Scandinavian influence," Tante suggested. "That longing for a color."

Robin pictured her grandmother stumping through the Better Dress Department, surveying herself in burgundy and grape in the three-way mirror, then crumpling to the floor in cardiac arrest. She pictured the harried salesperson, probably an elderly woman in reduced circumstances, sending for the buyer. The buyer inspecting the heap of this unknown woman on the Bonwit Teller carpet. The summons to the police, their discreet arrival by the service entrance, and the unceremonious carting away of her stricken grandmother by police ambulance. If it had happened in Charles Sumner's or Jacques or the Snooty Fox! If it had only happened in Makanna's, Shreve's, or the Swiss Boutique! What consternation, what elaborate emergency measures for Mrs. Brooks Latham. The smelling salts. The glass of bitters, the respectful doormen. The salesladies to smooth out her dress, straighten her wig, chafe her wrists. Dear Mrs. Latham. Poor Mrs. Latham. She shook herself. Would it always be her nature to worry a thought this way, fastening into it like a dog with a bone clamped in his teeth? Gran was dead, had fallen mercifully unconscious in that first swoon, had no need of her misgivings, second thoughts, regrets. Besides, there was Tante to consider, Tante now peering nearsightedly at the little clump of jewels, fingering the brooch. And tomorrow there would be Beth, her own true mother, who was after all the immediate bereaved.

"Suppose I fix us an omelette?" she asked Tante. "A big omelette with cheese? We have to eat something."

"Runny," Tante said cheerfully. "I do like my eggs on the runny side. To the horror of your grandmother." She checked herself.

Robin thought, *but we will always be conspirators.*

Beth and nurse Gloria, impeccably groomed for mourning, arrived the next day. They both sported bronze Lake Placid tans and black linen summer-resort dresses, and when Robin embraced her mother, the familiar brown medicinal smell of whiskey lurked under the perfume. By noon it was sweltering. During calling hours at the funeral home, which was only modestly cooled, Robin thought, we are true British colonials outfitted for the occasion. The funeral service was private. Afterward, a pitiful trickle of the Old Guard came and went. Robin gave and received the dry nonkisses of greeting and condolence. Her mother, she noticed, forestalled these by going at people with both hands extended. Tante was somewhat less embraced. Gloria kept demurely to one side.

They had the funeral meats. There were sherry and port on the sideboard. "Your grandmother was the secret benefactress of thousands," a little tissue-paper lady told Robin. "Thousands!" They had been members of the Tuesday Morning Club for forty years. A trustee of the Florence Crittenden Home said, "I knew your grandparents through three wars. They stood for something." The new minister and his wife went through a series of awkward greetings, like last-minute house guests. Gran had not appeared in church since three ministers ago; still, Tante had counseled and Robin agreed, it was best to observe

the proprieties. "To age-old things, their due," Tante had said
a little merrily. She was no longer the poor relation. At last she
was above the salt.

On the obituary page of the *Boston Globe,* Mrs. Brooks Latham was accorded the left-hand column. Respectful mention
was made of her philanthropies and memberships, and a Bach-
rach portrait dating from the fifties was also run. Two inches
sufficed in *The New York Times.* An era had ended.

Beth and Gloria took up residence again on the third floor.
Now there was liquor on the sideboard, not in decanters but in
raw bottles that said Johnny Walker or Smirnoff. Beer in the
refrigerator. Meals at odd hours, pizza on the Duncan Phyfe
dining table. An indifferent swipe at dust, a casual disorganiza-
tion. Gloria abandoned her uniform in favor of slacks that
ballooned like Turkish pajamas. She carried Beth's breakfast up
to her in midmorning; Robin seldom saw her mother before
noon. They deferred to each other in everything with the exaggerated care of dogs from different territories.

The house itself seemed to respond with new saggings. An
attic window now admitted pigeons. They could be heard cooing at dawn. There was a suspicious brown stain on the living-
room ceiling; somewhere a slow leak was working its way outward like a boil. And the front steps of herringbone brick, where
Gran had been ever vigilant, seemed now to invite a luxuriance
of weeds which sprang up in the cracks overnight.

The soul had fled. The soul, something as small as an apple
seed, perhaps, did not yield itself upon dissection. Robin had
read somewhere that a Swedish doctor had weighed the death-
beds of his terminal patients just before and after they lost their
vital signs. There was a twenty-one-gram difference. Unac-
countable to science, that three-quarters of an ounce, surely the

net weight of the soul now wafting about somewhere. Reabsorbed, probably, in the atmosphere, which would by now be clotted with the wisps of all the departed. As a child she had concluded that the soul was another organ, like a kidney or an ovary, which you might or might not have. Depending? Depending on whether you were made right. Live right to be made right, although of course that was backward. And keep your fingers out of all holes.

After a torment of ambivalence, Robin moved into her grandmother's bedroom. There was no reason to stay in the back storage room, still crammed with her childhood and the childhood of her mother. She slept sweetly reconciled in the dead woman's bed, woke to finger the familiar blue silk blanket cover, padded barefoot across the old comforting Chinese rug, ran her fingertips over the enduring bathroom tiles, square and yellow as horses' teeth. She found she could wash with Gran's lemon verbena soap and brush her teeth with Gran's leftover Dr. Lyon's tooth powder. Her image looked back dispassionately from the mirror that had for so long reflected only the outline of her grandmother. Robin Parks of sound mind and desirous young body. She had burst the envelope of the matriarch and slipped herself inside, and no evil had befallen. Moreover, she had fetched Dusty from New Hampshire, where Muhner had looked after him, and made a bed for him under the grand piano. He quivered with terror on the city streets. She got up early to take him for a daily run along the river. She was waiting to see. She could not have said for what. Something was gaining on her. A beaver dam flooded Mink Hill in her dream.

A week after the funeral, Robin was taken to lunch by Walter Hammersmith of Dale and Horn, her grandmother's law firm. He was a broad-hipped, assured man in his late sixties, with a

ruddy complexion and imposing white eyebrows. "A very determined lady," he told Robin over the chef's salad and Melba
toast. "Knew her for twenty years. She was a great believer in
rising to the occasion. I never saw her falter." After the Jell-O
and coffee—a spinster conclusion to a niggardly meal, Robin
thought it—they repaired to the bank vault. Hammersmith
stood by as Robin fitted the key in the safe-deposit box.

Before all else, there was a letter. "I will wait out front while
you read it," he said, semaphoring with the eyebrows. "She was
very intense; intense, not distraught, the day she wrote it. In my
office, in fact. Although not necessarily with my approval."

Robin sat in the little cubicle provided. The letter was dated
two years earlier. Gran had never been one to be caught una-
ware.

My dear Binnie:

By the time this letter is opened and read in the presence of
my lawyer, I will have completed my assigned journey and
you will commence to speak of me in the past tense. Perhaps
you will be in your mid-twenties, perhaps thirty, though that
is hardly likely. In any case, it is not given to me to know and
it is idle to speculate. I believe in the judicious exercise of my
authority and I must put my trust in Providence and the
guiding arm of Dale and Horn to implement it.

It is my fondest wish that you shall marry someone suitable,
as yet unknown to me, and that your unrealized or still postponed ambitions will come true. Whatever career you pursue,
I should like to think from beyond the grave that there will
be children and that you will bring them up wisely and com-
passionately to make something of themselves and to honor

their commitment as human beings in the race. Which is precisely what I have tried to do in the highly abnormal role of second motherhood that was thrust upon me. Perhaps your mother's unfortunate tendency has its roots in something I failed to do in the first instance. If so, it was out of ignorance rather than malice.

Although you are still at this writing a somewhat headstrong and willful young woman, I am naming you my sole heir and beneficiary of the estate left by your grandfather. I cannot in all conscience expect your mother to cope with the stresses this not inconsiderable inheritance imposes, but it goes without saying that you will sustain her and your great-aunt as long as this is necessary.

I trust that you will not waste your good energies in long and unnecessary grieving. One is gradually prepared for the responsibilities of adulthood. It is a negation of love to act otherwise. In the short time that remains to me I cherish the thought that you will not disappoint me.

Your loving grandmother

It was signed and witnessed. It was an official document. To Robin it was a totally unacceptable throw of the dice.

"Would you like to come back to the office to discuss this?" Hammersmith asked as he guided her by the elbow up out of the vault, into the sunlight.

She shook her head.

"We might walk up Tremont to the Common," he persisted. "I really think we should spend some time together to talk about the . . . ramifications. Binnie," he added. "Although we've just met, I hope you don't mind. I think of you as Binnie."

"What I'd like is a drink. For the first time in my life, what I'd really like is a drink."

He looked at her doubtfully.

"Don't worry," she said. "I am not predisposed, I promise you."

"I have a granddaughter your age," he said.

"Mr. Hammersmith . . ."

"Yes?"

"I need to sit down. In a dark place. On a chair. With a drink."

They went into the Parker House, unaccustomed as he was. It was decently dark in the lounge.

"Surely you expected . . ." he began.

"That she would die? That I would have to do the burying? Listen, I used to worry a lot, supposing she dies in bed, where will I find a doctor to come and certify that she's dead? She's gone up and down the Back Bay wearing out prominent specialists. Of course she was never very sick, but once she broke a bone in her foot and she sacked five orthopedic men in a row because they all told her not to put *any* weight on it. Finally she found one sly old fox who understood she had to be in charge. He told her she could put twenty per cent of her weight on it for two weeks. It was just enough. I used to think, well, I could call *him,* but he moved away, he went to New York."

Hammersmith made an appropriate noise.

"I mean, you knew her for twenty years, but you don't know anything, really. She never let anyone in. Everything went unexplained. I was probably eleven or twelve before I found out that my mother was a hopeless drunk, all along she was supposed to have a weak chest or something. I was fifteen before I caught on to the fact that my grandmother wasn't some sort of American countess bred to a strain of Boston Brahmins. I mean, she lived in the country of disdain, Gran did, but she had the secret heart of a commoner. She pretended she was raised in a castle and teethed on a gold bracelet when she really grew up next to a henhouse and went barefoot all summer to save on shoe leather. And all those things about my great-aunt, the whole vendetta over Uncle Davis and how Tante was an unsuitable match for him and how he was a moral weakling and she encouraged him in his faults, all of that. Responsibility and commitment! She was the upper hand, up over God. Believe me, Mr. Hammersmith, if my grandmother fell into a pickle barrel, she'd make you believe it was Ma Griffe, or something."

"But Binnie."

"Damn her, the old bitch! She just took a dump truck and dropped a load of shit all over my life. Damn her for dying. And you know, I loved her, for all her dowager spite, I really loved her."

Walter Hammersmith said a surprising thing. "What is love?" and signaled the waitress for another round.

"Well, I won't do it," Robin said. "I'll get rid of it. I'll give it away. I am not going to carry that inheritance around on my back, how much did you say it was?"

"A million dollars, in very round figures."

"Oh my God."

"It accumulates, you see."

"Well, I won't do it. I'm not even in charge of myself, let alone taking on the whole dynasty of the Lathams."

"I married for money," Walter Hammersmith said very clearly. "Thirty-five years ago I turned my back on love and I married for money. Position," he gestured. "A house on the North Shore. A mooring at the Yacht Club."

"Will you help me give it away?"

"I don't sail any more and I miss it," Hammersmith said. "I have prostate trouble, I have to have an operation. I'm terrified, I don't mind telling you."

Robin leaned across the table, waiting to get his attention. "*How do I get rid of it? Will you tell me?*"

"Every precaution has been taken," he said. "Your grandmother was a very charitable woman. She has spread gifts over her lifetime, established endowments, made generous bequests, and so on. I can assure you, the tax burden has been kept to the allowable minimum."

"You make it sound like a social virtue, all that storing up. I don't see any virtue in inherited wealth."

"Life is a series of nasty compromises." He blew his nose heavily. "The girl I loved had a nervous breakdown. She married an accountant. He handled some affairs for the firm. As a result, I saw her every quarter. They lived in Fall River until she died. She became terribly obese. Year after year she gained twenty pounds. And do you know why?"

"No. Why?"

"Despair. She became trapped in her despair. The girl I loved, trapped inside her . . . tonnage."

"You see," Robin said. "You'll have to help me."

"Your grandmother was a very regal person. Formidable in her insistence. I prided myself on our relationship. Others found her difficult. I always felt that she was rather lonely."

Robin began to like him.

"After Emily died—Emily was her name—I felt I couldn't go on. I felt that I was living a charade, a terrible charade, mourning for my mistress in Fall River and going home each night to Magnolia. One day at lunch, I never drink, I am by inclination a teetotaller, as you see, but your grandmother was feeling festive and she insisted, I had two Scotch mists and poured out the whole story. Like today. I was obsessed with this notion: Emily is dead. Emily stood between me and death. I'm next. And do you know what she said to me?"

"No. What?"

"She said, 'Nonsense, Walter. You're not going to die. Life is a cold duty and you must see me through.' "

Robin shook her head grimly. "It sounds just like her."

"And I took great comfort from it," he went on. "Great comfort. It meant that I was still a father and a husband in the widest sense. And now I must see you through."

"All right," she said. "Where do we begin?"

"Begin what?"

"Giving it away."

"My dear Binnie," and it was her grandmother's voice she heard, "this is not a game of cards or pocket billiards. You cannot simply dissipate an inheritance by giving it away. Manage it, yes, make certain adjustments or reinvestments, perhaps establish a separate trust to cover your poor mother's annual expenses. But to talk of giving it away, that is foolish idealism. Childish in the extreme."

She drained her drink. "I am a retired child. And that's how it's going to be."

"I am prepared to advise you, do whatever legal work is required to redistribute the estate your grandfather left in trust, but you must be reasonable."

"Mr. Hammersmith, what is reasonable by my lights and what is reasonable by your lights are . . . are . . ."

"Incompatible?"

She found her word. "Irreconcilable."

"You must not hold money in contempt," he told her gravely. "After all, you have enjoyed the fruits of it all your life. You've lived . . ."

" 'In a bright light, in houses of pearl and porcelain,' " she said. "Thoreau said that. He said we drink only light wines, our teeth are set on edge by the least natural sour, do you know what that means?"

"I hardly see . . ."

"I thought you might," she said. "I thought after what you told me about living a terrible charade that you might understand."

But his moment in the confessional had passed. "I want to protect you from making a terrible mistake. You have no right to squander the inheritance of generations."

"You're fired," she said.

He smiled; a contained, angry show of teeth. "I'm afraid that's not possible."

"Are you telling me I can't hire and fire my own legal advisers?"

"You can't fire me, my dear, because I haven't been hired. My legal services terminated with the death of your grandmother."

She didn't understand. "But what about today?"

He was taking out his wallet, counting out the tip. "Today was a courtesy. A courtesy in the widest sense, in memory of a gallant lady."

❋ "WELL, WHAT DID old Hammer and Sickle say?" Beth asked. "Come in, come in, join the party." She was wearing a yellow negligee and a yellow hair ribbon and sat tucked up on the sofa, hugging her knees to her chest. Her toenails were bright pink. She had the small folded look of a butterfly against the damask. "We're having screwdrivers, the orange juice is freshly squozen. Make yourself a drink, join the crowd."

The crowd was Gloria, also in a negligee, a spatter of red peonies on a black ground. "Afternoon naps," she explained. "Your mother sleeps so lightly at night that I encourage her to catch forty winks. Oh, and your great-aunt called. I told her you had a business appointment."

"Binnie darling." Beth patted a space on the sofa. "*Do* come and sit down. Tell us all the news."

"I have to walk the dog first."

"It's too late," Gloria said. "He already made a big b.m. in the kitchen."

"I'm sorry you had to clean it up."

"As a matter of fact, I didn't. I thought you might want to show it to him. I mean, he's your dog."

Robin turned on her heel. "It is also my house."

"All the more reason," Gloria called gaily to her retreating back.

Robin turned back. "All the more reason for me to choose my own house guests, too."

From the kitchen she could hear the onset of a quarrel. "I just think it would be, that's all." "You just think, you just think!" "You don't have one ounce of humility in your veins." "Maybe not. I know something else you have in yours." Like cats squaring off on the back fence. She sighed, scooped up the turd onto the morning section of the *Times,* and carried it out back to the trash can. Out of the corner of her eye she saw something flick past in the alley. It could have been a squirrel or a bird, but she knew she had seen a rat.

At the river she let Dusty run free, flushing pigeons. She headed up the lagoon while he raced along the bank, plunging in the water to drive a cluster of ducks farther offshore. From a safe distance they formed a vee and quacked at him. He shook himself delightedly, then bounded back to her, the plume of his tail thrashing like a metronome. There were other walkers by the river that early fall afternoon, all of them in pairs, with the wind catching in their shirttails and tumbling their hair into their eyes. They walked side by side without touching or skipped stones or else they moved bearlike, arms lacing them together to form one outline. There were couples out sailing and couples on the grass, and then there was Robin Parks saddled with her hypothetical moneybag and her unhousebroken puppy.

She put Dusty back on the leash and walked back down along the lagoon, threaded across the Drive, and started up Beacon Hill.

Tante too was on the sofa. She ventured out hardly at all, complaining of the unseasonable heat of September, the excessive traffic, the terrible demands of her pupils, who arrived thoughtlessly late or called at the last minute to cancel. Her composure, which had not cracked at all in the first days of the death and rearrangements, now seemed threatened. Gran's Friday-afternoon seat at the Symphony was hers. The Theatre Guild tickets had fallen to her. The City Club had requested that she take the other Mrs. Latham's place on its education committee. The Museum Board would like to know if she was willing to fill her sister-in-law's unexpired term. Gran's absence was like a missing tooth; the tongue obsessionally probes the gap. "Will they leave me no cud to chew?" she complained to Robin.

"I've seen Dale and Horn," Robin said.

"Poor Binnie! You with those stocks and bonds and codicils all day. And here I've been rattling on like an old tin Lizzie. Was it awful?"

"Did you know she was going to do it?"

"Did I know she was going to do what?"

"Leave it all to me."

There was a long pause before Tante spoke. Then she said, "I never doubted it for a moment. *Pas une minute.* Oh, she set herself in judgment from the first, Lydia did, she took some primitive pleasure from her casting off. Your poor mother was doomed from the cradle. It was not a wholesome atmosphere, Brooks doting and dandling and your grandmother glowering and resenting. Do you remember *mirror, mirror on the wall?*"

Robin nodded. She remembered especially the heart, salted and cooked, but she said nothing.

"That's what it was, Binnie. A dreadful contest from the first. The blindness of parents! My heart ached for Beth, she came to me as often as she was allowed, we shared our little secrets all through her girlhood. Although she was never as close to me, Binnie, as you have been. She had such thorns, you see. To protect from more hurt."

"I just don't know what to do," Robin said. "It's such a mess. Of course, Mother will be furious. She and Gloria are lying about, toasting each other, waiting for the spoils. The division of parts."

Tante made a large gesture in the air. "Divest yourself, dear. Sell the house. It's a dreadful white elephant nowadays, perhaps some secretarial school can be persuaded to buy it."

"Mother seems to want to stay there," Robin suggested.

"Now Binnie, we both know how that will end. Your mother and that dreadful Miss Barnum—Lydia was right about *her*, at any rate—will simply reduce the furnishings to a shambles. For one thing, I am sure I detected mice in the pantry. That afternoon after the funeral when I was shunted aside . . ."

Robin made sounds of demurral.

"Nevertheless, I kept to the background. Discretion, Binnie.

I know my place. I've practiced it for years. But that afternoon, passing between the kitchen and the parlor, I could not keep from feeling something in the air. Something . . . abnormal in their relationship. I mean, it transcends what is to be expected of a friendship between two mature women."

"Does it matter?" Robin asked. "If they're happy together?"

"One does not like to see that sort of thing made public. Bruited about. But the worst of it is, I feel that Miss Barnum has come between your mother and me. To a significant degree."

When you are a child, Robin thought, you see like a horse with blinders. Tunnel vision, but direct, and safe. The world is starched and white, as if made of sheets hung out. Now everything was naked to behold. The rods and cones took in an immense landscape. Slag piles and trash heaps. Her head ached from the afternoon at the Parker House. "Let's cheer each other up," she said. "Let's have a wicked cocktail out of your special glasses."

Tante brightened. "We just might get a little tipsy together."

They settled into the oh-so-carefully-measured Dubonnet and gin. Robin swirled the stem of her glass and looked through the rosy liquid at the room. How many times, she thought. How many times. Dusty scratched round and round in a corner by the bookcase, then fell asleep on his back, legs askew in the air. The pink undersides of his jowls fluttered as he breathed.

"I'm on the scrap heap, Binnie," Tante said midway in the second drink. "The golden years are just a sentimental lie. I've been segregated, as if old age were a contagion. At my age one is supposed to enjoy the company of the other old crones. The ones who don't die outright go off to nursing homes to live like dolls in a doll house. They are homesick children away at boarding school. They are talked about not only behind their backs, which after all one could tolerate, having done it, but to their faces as if they were faces without ears. I don't want to go that route, Binnie. Promise me that."

"Don't even think it!"

"I must think it. My eyesight is failing me fast, I can't go on pretending much longer, Binnie. Even with this"—she gestured at the magnifying glass—"it is an effort to make out more than the headlines. Sometimes on the street I get muddled; is it Boston? or Berlin? The street signs seem to be in some unintelligible language. I hardly dare venture out on a gray day, I'm deathly afraid of losing my way and being carted off like Mrs. Bagley."

Mrs. Bagley had been Gran's housekeeper, light-years ago. She wore pins and needles in the lapel of her uniform and she beat at the tops of the velvet curtains with an orange yardstick to dislodge "the black widders." When she left, five spoons and a carving knife vanished with her. Her niece reported her missing. The police found her in a rooming house in East Boston a week later, but she no longer knew who she was.

"Mrs. Bagley was always nutty as a fruitcake," Robin said. "Remember the leg of lamb in the linen closet, all tucked up in a blanket?"

"She said she felt sorry for it," Tante added. They giggled.

"But all the same," Robin said. "You could have a companion. That's no disgrace. Someone to be your eyes."

"Never." Tante was firm. "No, one day, God willing, I'll just roll over and die. After all, it's only bad magic to shrink from it. Death is the one fresh experience left, Binnie, there's something cozy about it. Part of it is comfy and warm, a promise, a nanny in a gray cape or the sort of greatcoat the Russians wore in the Crimean War, all flapping from the waist to the boottops. No, don't shrink from it, let me tell you the truth. Don't be afraid of me when I'm dead. I'll be cold to the touch—like soapstone, I suppose—"

Robin buried her face in her hands.

"I know you think I'm being morbid. But I want to tell you now, while I have my wits left. Time no longer stretches before me like a good elastic band, Binnie. The day loses its boundary. I find now I sleep any which way. Morning, night, they have no meaning. And I populate the night with what are known as daydreams. My body disgusts me."

"I'm not listening!"

"My body disgusts me, it still has its appetites and no one, no way to satisfy them. I dream of Davis and Axel and of a dear young man I knew once in Paris who held me in his arms one whole night. I dream all the cities of my past and in my dreams I am forever young. I mix up times, and places, they all run together like a water color. I know I can live only one day at a time. You're no different from me in that respect, at least. But my day is peopled with the deaths of others. All my dead friends have taken away a piece of myself in their dying. Here a fingernail, there a morsel. It's a kind of irreversible leprosy."

"Oh, Tante," Robin said tearfully, "I'm so sorry! I'm so sorry you have to get old."

But the monologue had made Tante cheerful. "Don't you cry over me, Binnie, not as long as I have breath to complain. No, I'll hold my life open as long as the latch will stand. There's a little self-pity in all of us, you know. It was nothing—a touch of the *cafard*." They embraced. Robin whistled her dog awake and walked back, skirting the Common, to the house on Marlborough Street.

✳ 10 ✳

The Uterus Tree

SOMEWHERE PAST midnight, Robin woke to the sound of rain. It was not a steady drumming, which might have been comforting, but a series of metallic rattles, followed by the whoosh of wind gusts. Then an interval of suspended calm, then the tinny presence again. The dream she struggled up from was as static as a stage set before the characters begin to speak. It was the strawberry field, the horses grazing in the center. She and David sat under the Uterus Tree. It was not unlike a basswood in full blossom, the droning of the bees in it erupting finally into the reality of the rain. In the dream David had not yet asked her what kind of a tree it was, but the lines had been written and the answer had formed in her sleeping mind. The Uterus Tree was a family tree, its forks were family feelings, its flowers and leaf plates were genes and blood lines. The shapes of noses, the smell and clutch of the past. Why David? she wondered. Once, trying to explain the fascination the diaries and journals of the first settlers held for her, she had said to Jeff: I come from an old family. He had thrown back his head and laughed. *Our families undoubtedly came down out of the trees within weeks of each other,* he'd said. Of course hers were written down in church records and old Bibles, and his had been lost in mystery. Stamped out in the Crusades, or burned out by the Cossacks. *But we all started out with the same monkey wit,* he'd told her. Monkey wit, like motherwit. Did it mean she would never sit under the Uterus Tree with Jeff? That she might have, with David? Who after all, in the manner of the family tree, drank too much?

The rain rattled again, like hailstones on iron. She went out into the hall, then down into the dining room, tracking the sound, switching on lights as she passed. There was a little pile of cardboard cartons on the table, attesting to Chinese food sent in from the Green Jade. She crossed the hall and circled the living room, looking up. There it was. The brown stain, now widened like a squashed mushroom, had finally burst into a leak. It was dripping in fierce little intermittent freshets onto a bronze tea chest. Relieved that the infection had now localized, she went to fetch a pot. The leak still pinged on metal, so she stuffed a kitchen towel in the bottom and listened, head cocked. That did it. She surmised that water was coming in under the eaves, blown in by the northeast wind. Squirrels must have chewed a corner there. Or rats. Rats don't climb like that, or do they?

"So we're coming apart at the seams," Beth said, behind her.

The unexpected voice made her jump. "What are you doing up?" she asked her mother.

"Same thing you are, I guess."

"I heard the dripping," Robin explained.

"I know. I couldn't sleep."

"What's wrong?"

"Oh, just one of my white nights." She emptied the dregs of

a whiskey glass into the pot, then uncapped the Scotch. "Join me?"

Robin shook her head.

"Well, stay with me a little while, will you, darling? I'm awfully blue."

Robin sat down in an armchair. Dusty came out from under the piano and sat with his chin in her lap. She stroked his head, aware of the fragile triangulation of his skull. With a hammer you could smash it, like that. He sighed his gratitude.

"I know what you're thinking," Beth said. "You're thinking what a lush your mother is."

"It's your life."

"Meaning you don't give a damn."

"No. Meaning I can't keep you from killing yourself with booze."

"Well, why shouldn't I? Is it any better to drop dead in Bonwit Teller instead?"

"Gran didn't drop dead at forty-seven. She led a long and what she would have called a useful life."

Beth snorted. "A useful life. Years of boredom interrupted by ugly surprises. When the commoners rebelled against the empress."

Robin ran her hand lightly over the dog's face. He submitted, blinking only mildly as her fingers passed across his eyes. A pinch between thumb and forefinger, you could snuff out sight as simply as a candle flame.

"Go ahead," Beth said. "Judge me. Judge me with your disapproving silence. You don't have to tell me what a rotten mother I've been, what a trial, what a blot on the family name. Well, let me tell you a few things. Your saintly grandmother would have driven anyone to drink. As it was, she only got to Daddy and me."

"I'm not blaming you."

"Well, *she* did. She found fault with every single thing I did in my life, except maybe having you."

Robin remembered the letter. *Highly abnormal second motherhood,* Gran had said. "It wasn't exactly a picnic for me, either. The leftover child."

"Oh, darling, don't you think I know that? Don't you think I've killed myself a thousand times over what I did to you?"

"You're being very dramatic," Robin said. "For the fifth act."

"Don't you think I despise myself for the way things turned out? That I have some capacity left for caring? If only I'd had a little more courage, or if only Daddy had been a little stronger."

"Grandpa?"

"Yes, Grandpa. My father. You hardly remember him," Beth said. "But he adored me. I was his poppet, his lambkin, his Little Miss Muffet. He had such faith in me! He always said I could do anything, I could be anybody I wanted to. He was such a handsome man, it's a pity you don't remember. Tall and straight and with a marvelous twinkle. Even though he drank. He hid it, it was part of his private nature, nipping away in pantries and stopping off at his club. I'd catch him on the back stairs with a bottle and he'd wink and say, 'Our secret, Poppet.' I don't think she ever really realized. She didn't want to. After all, he was quite a catch, she liked to show him off, like a Ming vase. But she couldn't bear to share him. She couldn't forgive him for getting her pregnant and then she couldn't share him. In the end, she made him choose. She made my Daddy choose."

"Maybe it seemed that way. Maybe it always seems that way when you're little."

"Seemed! She couldn't wait to unload me, marry me off, get me out of the house. I had him absolutely by heart, I never forgot him, never. Even after Roger was killed in Korea and I went through the first bad time, Daddy stayed. He was the cleanest man I ever saw. He buffed his own fingernails and afterward he ran this little white string under them. I can still dream about him. In my dreams he's always the same. The good dreams, anyhow."

"You're lucky. I never had enough father to dream about."

"Well, you never had bad chloral dreams either, baby. So it evens out."

"Is that what they give you in those places? Chloral?"

"The therapy of choice," Beth said. "In addition to always being in the country, as if green grass and brown cows could make you want to drink less. Chloral keeps the decibel level down at night. No wonder I can't sleep here, it's so damn quiet. Nobody moaning or crying. And when you get to be a pill hoarder—when you tuck them in your cheek and pretend to swallow them—they give it to you in liquid form. To make sure you swallow it then, you see. It's nice that way. More of a rush."

"But it gives you nightmares, is that it?"

"Correction. Life gives you nightmares. The dream machine grinds them out and you get up on stage and run through them."

"But when you drink you don't dream?"

"When you drink," Beth said, refilling her glass, "you don't feel."

"Did you drink like that when Daddy was alive?"

"Daddy Roger? Your Daddy, you mean?"

"There was such a man," Robin said. "Because I remember him, I remember his bow ties and a certain way he smelled."

"Smelled?"

"A kind of mixture, a hospital smell and tobacco."

"Ether," Beth said decisively. "He positively reeked of it. It's terribly drying, you know. I used to think the bed would explode. Blow up."

"You never talk about him," Robin prodded.

"Talk. What's there to say?"

"What he was like."

"He was young and ambitious. Even though he came from the Boston Parkses, he wanted to be a neurosurgeon. There were a lot of nights he never came home. He despised me for being lonely, for drinking when he was on duty fluttering the oxygen into other people's lungs. The bed was empty. It was a toy marriage, Mother pushed me into it."

"Didn't you push back?"

"Me? The spineless wonder? I didn't really mind. In the beginning it was lighthearted, it was fun being married, having a little baby. And then he was drafted, the doctor draft, and he went to Korea and was killed."

"That's very sad," Robin said, meaning *sad for me.* "Very goddam awfully sad."

"It was terrible. The worst of it was, instead of feeling relieved, I felt guilty."

"And what about me? You expected to feel relieved, didn't I deserve a father?"

"Oh, Binnie, don't you see? It just goes round and round. It was so rotten of me."

"Life is rotten," Robin relented. "After all, you didn't kill him."

"I might as well have. I think I'll freshen this. I think I'll have a drink on the house."

"That's fine," Robin said. "Go ahead. Meanwhile the house is falling down around our ears."

"Let it fall. Let the old mausoleum fall down like London Bridge."

"I've been meaning to talk to you about that. I've been wanting to ask you, what are your plans?"

"My plans are to have this last little drink and toddle off to sleep."

"And tomorrow?"

Beth shrugged elaborately. The liquid sloshed in the glass. "Tomorrow never comes."

"Today, then," Robin said grimly. "You and Gloria better start packing. Because this is the end of the line. I'm going to put the house on the market. I'm going to sell it off now before the whole roof blows away."

"You mean you'd throw me out of my own house, just like that? Throw your own mother out?"

"After all you've done for me, is that what you mean? After you gave me the best years of your life, is that the way it goes?"

"God. You're just like your grandmother. The same terrible sarcasm. She never touched me, except with words. She broke my back with words, and you're just like her, Binnie. She taught you how."

Robin, contrite, pushed the dog aside and went over to her mother. She was not up to a full-scale hug, but squeezed her shoulder; aware, too, how fragile the bone structure; how narrow, how defeated. "I didn't mean it to sound like that. You're right, it scares me, I open my mouth and Gran's voice comes out. She was queen of the cutting remark, we both know that."

Beth wept a little. "We can compare our scars."

"But I loved her. And you did, too, once. You must have. We're the same blood, the same biology." Pleading, *Please say you loved her, please say it was all worth something.*

But the tears were maudlin now. "I loved Daddy. And Daddy left me out."

"Okay, but that was long ago. They're both dead, Gran and Grandpa, the house is falling down. It would be decent if we could talk this over."

"Talk! Talk! I know she left it all to you. I always knew she was going to."

"But I promise to take care of you. I promise that you and Gloria can live happily ever after as long as you want. You can travel, there'll always be a penthouse, the best liquor, and when you want them, the best sans. Arizona, California, Greece, wherever. I'll put enough in trust, enough for you to live on, and Tante too, whatever she needs. Remember how you loved Tante once? Remember how you used to go there and talk and listen to music, the same way I did? I learned it from you. You showed me where to go, where it was holy and safe."

"Mother and Daddy left me out," Beth was saying, "but Robin let me in." She wobbled across the room. "Christ, I feel sad. Oh, Christ, I'm going to throw up."

"Go to bed," Robin said, steering her. "Let's wake up Gloria, she'll tuck you in." And helped her broken mother up two flights.

Downstairs again, she emptied the pot, reset it under the staccato drip, and poured herself three fingers of Scotch. "I'm tying them on three in a row," she said to the dog. "Drinking with the lawyer, the old auntie, the little mother."

After a while, she got up and went in search of a pen and a

pad of paper. "First you have to straighten out all your premises and *a priori's*," she said aloud, and Dusty, between dozes, thumped his tail. "1. 'Doing-good is one of the professions that are full.' 2. 'Spend the nine-tenths and be done with it.' 3. 'Rescue the drowning and tie your shoestrings.' "

At the top of the list, she wrote: THE GIVEAWAYS. Angell Memorial Hospital. "That's in your name," she told the dog. She thought, drank, then wrote under it, Anti-Vivisection Society, Boston Eye Bank, Common Cause. Day Care Centers. Ecology, Inc. Fortune Society, Four-H-Clubs, Friends of the Earth, Glaucoma Institute, and so on, down through Vietnam Veterans Against the War and Welfare Mothers.

In the morning she walked up Commonwealth Avenue to a used-car agency and bought a five-year-old Jeep. The brakes needed relining, the tires were bald, but the motor, they assured her, as she revved it, killed it, restarted, listened critically to it idling, the motor was in excellent condition. Buying the Jeep made her feel positively lightheaded. She could not have said where she was going, only that she could now carry her house on her back.

In the afternoon she went to Dale and Horn. Mr. Hammersmith took her into his office, where she was touched to see pots of nasturtiums growing on the window sill. "I'm going to try to winter them over," he said. "They're very undemanding."

Robin agreed. She considered telling him they were good to eat, too, leaf and bud, but thought better of it. "I want to apologize for yesterday. For . . . presuming that way."

He pressed his fingertips together to make a little church. "I knew you could be trusted to take hold."

"Don't misunderstand me. I haven't changed my mind."

"Perhaps when the first shock has passed?"

She shook her head. "I will need the will, a list of the securities, and so on."

"There never was an Emily," he said harshly. "Do you hear me? Emily was purely an invention. Of my overworked imagination."

"Also, I'm going to sell the house. I'll need an agent."

"Those fine old houses." He mourned.

"They leak. They're draughty, the plumbing breaks down, and there are rats in the alley."

"Oh, surely not rats?"

"Mr. Hammersmith, I want you to know that I respect the privacy of our earlier conversations. I can keep a confidence. And I will expect you to charge me for today's interview."

"If you insist on behaving so irresponsibly . . ."

"It's not irresponsible. It's vital."

"You leave me no choice. I can't throw you to the wolves. You, the granddaughter of Lydia Latham. I will stay on as your attorney." He unmade the church of his fingers and rose from the desk to take her two hands in his.

❋ "DARLING, I'VE FOUND the most marvelous place," Gloria was saying. "It's in Arizona, a desert condominium, all air-conditioned and with swimming pools and tennis courts. They have horses, too, and tons of Indian ruins."

It could have been Gran.

The two women were packing.

"Of course you should take it with you," Robin said of the silver tea service, the domed serving platters, the candelabra, the Persian miniatures, the Sargent original. She said "of course" to the Aubusson, the tea chest, the Chinese lamps.

The divesting went forward slowly. The roofer came wearing his most funereal expression. His brother-in-law was an exterminator. No use to put the house on the market until the pigeons had been dealt with, the squirrels removed. The rats in the alley were out of his province.

"There should have been a preconceived plan," Hammersmith lamented at Dale and Horn. "There will be difficult liquidity problems, it should all have been coordinated into a strong economic unit."

Robin sympathized.

"Reticence—your grandmother had a penchant for secretiveness—reticence is the arch enemy of planning. What we have here is a hodgepodge. I'm afraid we're in for a real tax extravagance."

"Well, we have to give the government its due," she said cheerfully. "How else can they afford to make war?"

Hammersmith was not amused. "Now Binnie. I make it a practice never to discuss politics with a client."

Just get rid of it, she urged him silently.

❋ AND THEN THERE was Jeff calling from New York. She and Beth and Gloria were eating Colonel Sanders' fried chicken out of a cardboard drum. Bits of the breading were scattered on the Duncan Phyfe table. She carried a wing with her when she went to answer the phone.

"Poor Robinowitz! I just got in. I just got in tonight from Canada. Muhner told me about your grandmother. I tried to call you there just now, and he told me. It must have been a nightmare for you."

"Yes," she said. Anything else would have stuck in her throat.

"Have you got a cold or something? Are you crying? You don't sound like yourself."

"Who do I sound like?"

"I don't know. Greta Garbo, for Christ's sake! Robinowitz. It's *me,* Jeff. I want to come see you. When should I come? Should I come up tonight?"

She was silent for a long time; she could hear him breathing, which meant he could hear her breathing too, into the mouthpiece. "How about some time next week?" she finally said.

"Next *week?* Are you crazy? I can't wait till next week."

"I'm really awfully busy. I mean the roofer and the exterminator and everything."

"What the hell are you exterminating?"

"The estate. Mother and Gloria are moving to Phoenix. I'm selling the house and all that."

"Well, why the fuck do *you* have to do it?"

"Because," Robin said. "I am the immediate family, that's why."

"No, that's not what I mean. Didn't she have a will, or something?"

"She left it all to me. So that's why I'm so busy. I'm divesting myself."

Now he breathed, and she listened. Finally he said, "When do you think you'll be done divesting?"

"It's taking ages. I made a list of all the giveaways, it's in alphabetical order but first you have to determine the purchase price of the securities."

"Giveaways?"

"Organizations. To give money to. Like Operation Outreach for Problem Drinkers, Planned Parenthood, Quaker Hill School for Exceptional Children, Rescue, Incorporated . . ."

"What's that?"

"It's a suicide-prevention agency. Anyway, things like that. And then you have to determine the market price."

"It's very complicated," Jeff said.

"We are trying to avoid a tax extravagance."

"And still have something left."

"Jeff, you're not listening! Why don't you ever listen? The whole idea is to have nothing left! Do you hear me? Nothing!"

"I hear you, Robinowitz. Don't get all uptight with me."

"So you better not come till next week."

"What's the matter? You think I want to get on your list, is that it? You think I want to be one of your giveaways? I don't give a damn about your gold-plated securities, Robinowitz. You're the one I care about. You're all I want."

"I missed you," she said. "All summer I missed you terribly."

❊ HE TOOK THE NEXT plane to Boston. Beth and Gloria completed their inventory for the movers and went up to their third-floor suite. "So we won't be underfoot," Beth explained. "Anyway, my hair is a mess. Gloria's going to give me a protein shampoo."

Robin swept up the debris of their patchwork supper, checked the pantry for mouse droppings, and walked the dog. She turned on the hall light and the outside light and all the lights in the living room, and then she sat at the piano and watched the headlights of passing cars, which began at the corner as little dense circles and widened and diffused as they passed. Finally there was a taxi stopping. She ran out of the house and down the witchgrass-invaded walk and they hugged and laughed and tears ran down her cheeks on Marlborough Street.

They talked. They sat in the old brown kitchen, the wainscoting mustard-slick with varnish and the night sounds of small things scrabbling behind the walls, and they talked. Blackberries as big as plums in British Columbia, mosquitoes with the wing-

spread of robins. Fields of swallowtail butterflies. Unraveling a
sweater to make a fishing line. Starting a cooking fire in a
downpour. The way Muhner looked in his funny one-piece
underwear the day that Gran collapsed in Bonwit Teller. Also
the way he looked the day he gave Robin a puppy. The puppy,
who was now almost a dog, sat alongside Jeff's chair and rested
his chin on Jeff's lap. Erica and the house full of children. The
horses and the strawberry field. She did not mention David
Despery. She said nothing of the dream about the Uterus Tree.

They talked until they had said enough to look back at each
other, and went around switching off all the lights. And Jeffrey
Rabinowitz, who was not on the list, Jeffrey Rabinowitz, who
had never been abovestairs in Gran's house, now spent the night
naked in her high sleigh bed with her only designated heir.